W9-AZM-610

HARVEY AND THE EXTRAORDINARY

Eliza Martin
Illustrated by Anna Bron

annick
press
toronto · berkeley

Based on the play *Harvey and the Extraordinary*, written and performed by
Eliza Martin and directed by Neil Silcox.

Cover art by Anna Bron, designed by Paul Covello
Interior designed by Paul Covello
Edited by Claire Caldwell
Copyedited by Mary Ann Blair
Proofread by Eleanor Gasparik

Annick Press Ltd.

We acknowledge the support of the Canada Council for the Arts and the
Ontario Arts Council, and the participation of the Government of Canada/la
participation du gouvernement du Canada for our publishing activities.

Canadä

ONTARIO ARTS COUNCIL
CONSEIL DES ARTS DE L'ONTARIO
an Ontario government agency
un organisme du gouvernement de l'Ontario

Library and Archives Canada Cataloguing in Publication

Title: Harvey and the extraordinary / Eliza Martin ; illustrated by Anna Bron.
Names: Martin, Eliza, author. | Bron, Anna, 1989- illustrator.
Identifiers: Canadiana (print) 2021018860X | Canadiana (ebook) 20210188669 | ISBN 9781773215433
(hardcover) | ISBN 9781773215440 (softcover) | ISBN 9781773215464 (PDF) | ISBN 9781773215457
(HTML)
Classification: LCC PS8626.A769475 H37 2021 | DDC jC813/.6—dc23

FEB -   '22   Published in the U.S.A. by Annick Press (U.S.) Ltd.
Distributed in Canada by University of Toronto Press.
Distributed in the U.S.A. by Publishers Group West.

Printed in Canada

annickpress.com
elizamartin.ca
annabron.com

Also available as an e-book.
Please visit annickpress.com/ebooks for more details.

MIX
Paper from
responsible sources
FSC® C103567

In memory of my Papa Richard Fisher,
for his endless encouragement and
the gift of an imaginary friend named
Harvey, and my Papa Al Martin for
inspiring my wonder of the circus.
—E.M.

To my family.
—A.B.

Preshow

A hush falls over the crowd as the spotlight swings around to find him. He's standing at the bottom of a ladder. He breathes in and sets his foot on the first rung.

"Ladies and gentlemen! Children of all ages! Feast your eyes upon our next act!"

Step after step, the ladder takes him higher and higher up into the tent—until he can't smell the popcorn anymore and the faces below turn into far-off blurs.

"Heeeeee's fearless!"

He stops for a moment and squints, looking down at the sea of people below—in spinning technicolor. He keeps a steady rhythm. One foot, the next. One foot, the next.

"He's nothing like you've ever seen before!"

The tent falls silent as he reaches the top. He hears nothing but his own heartbeat. Shakily, he steps out onto the platform, his knees quivering. A murmur ripples through the crowd, and camera lights flash like tiny explosions through the big top. He moves slowly, arms outstretched, keeping himself balanced as he carefully steps up to the edge. He looks down and sees it, a tiny blue speck just under his toes—the pool of water he's about to dive into. The crowd oohs and aahs. Their laughter swirls, and he hears Grimaldi the Lion roar from his cage backstage.

He takes a deep breath.

"The one!"

He stops.

A memory hits him so hard that he doubles over with the heartache—the pain in his chest. The crowd gasps, and somewhere a woman screams. Quickly he lurches back upright. The show must go on!

"The only!"

For a second, he stands still and shuts his eyes. Willing the memories to leave. The laughter, the little hand in his. Big green eyes and freckles. He lifts his foot to step again but—not without her. Standing tall, worlds above the crowd, he thinks of the worn school picture. And there she is. His little girl—

A drumroll splits through the air.

"THE EXTRAORDINARY!"

He jumps.

Chapter One

There are very few truly extraordinary things in the world. You see, extraordinary is extremely rare. Extraordinary only comes around on a snow day, a cheap-movie Tuesday, or in a carton of cold chocolate milk. Extraordinary is the golden star on your book report, brightly painted toenails, and stained-glass windows in unexpected places. It can only be found in orange the fruit, not the color. It's as special as a blue-raspberry sour candy or the perfect horizontal-striped T-shirt, lovingly worn in and still warm from the dryer. The word *extraordinary* is extraordinary in itself because it ends in a Y, which is the only letter that has a tail. And only the most extraordinary animals have tails, so that's why it's a very extraordinary letter.

The way I woke up this morning, though? Completely extra-ordinary. The door sounded like it was going to split in half from the force of Dominic's knocking.

"WAAAKE UUUP!" he yelled.

I pulled the pillow over my face, breathing in floral-patterned flannel.

Extra-ordinary is a whole other word. Extra-ordinary isn't extraordinary at all—it's much, much worse. I mean, ordinary is okay, but extra-ordinary is extra okay. If you think about it, it's really, really bad. Extra-ordinary is your older brother pounding on your bedroom door like a woodpecker practicing Morse code at exactly seven thirty in the morning on your eleventh birthday.

"MIMIIIIII!"

Mimi, short for Miriam, is an extremely extra-ordinary named given to me by my great-aunt Miriam. Nothing extraordinary has ever been given by a great-aunt. Aside from dusty old names, great-aunts only give doilies, raisin oatmeal cookies you thought were chocolate chip, and fleece pajamas with itchy tags. Very extra-ordinary things indeed.

At least, that's what I've decided. Oh, and did I mention that I'm the chief authority on all things extraordinary because, you see, I invented Extraordinaryism? I'm an expert! That is, I have a long chart taped to my bedroom wall where I write down everything in my life as extra-ordinary, ordinary, or extraordinary. It looks like this:

EXTRA-ORDINARY	ORDINARY	EXTRAORDINARY
Bucket hats	Pumpkins	Ruffley umbrellas
Turnips	Irish dancing	Zebras
Falling asleep in movies	Principal Miller's coffee breath	Hawaiian pizza
Orange (color)	Back crawl	Orange (fruit)
Video games	Mom	Art class
Non-chocolate milk	Dominic	Orange (soda)
Raisins	Putting on sunscreen	Dad
Skateboarding ramps	Cheesecake	Painted toenails
Aunt Daphne's kisses	White chocolate	Turquoise

The truth is, I'm an expert because from the moment I was born, I was extraordinary. Everyone knew. At least, that's what my dad said. And here I was, eleven years later—still extraordinary but much taller, far more freckled, and with a neon-green cast on my right arm. My dad would know a thing or two about being extraordinary because, though I did invent the word Extraordinaryism, it was my dad who inspired it. Extraordinaryism doesn't have a lot of research behind it yet, but it must be at least partially genetic because I take after him. I'm sure he would do a better job of explaining it, too, but he's off being way too famous and extraordinary. By far the most extraordinary thing about me is that my dad is a *renowned* circus performer.

Having a famous dad changes a lot of things. Sometimes it means he won't be there for your birthday—at least not this year. But as a fellow extraordinary person, he knew I would understand.

Extraordinary people are made for something more. That's why they can never stay. That's the first rule of Extraordinaryism.

Maybe on a less extraordinary day the rude knocking would have dampened my spirits, but today was my special day, and nothing would stop me from enjoying it. I leapt out of bed.

After a careful peek into the hall to ensure Dominic had already gone, I threw open my bedroom door. As I reached the top of the stairs, I noticed a small, red paper arrow pointing down to the main floor. I smiled with delight. The best surprises are birthday surprises!

I raced down the stairs, collecting the arrows as I went, my bare feet making the old wooden steps creak. The arrows led me all the way into the bright-yellow kitchen, which was streaming with sunlight and looking, if possible, even more yellow than it normally did. Dominic was already seated at the table, frowning and eating his cereal. Next to him, directly in front of the last paper arrow on the counter, was a small cage. Dominic was shoveling spoonfuls of cereal into his mouth with one hand while the other was crammed into the side of the cage, fingers waggling. I skidded to a stop on a black-and-white tile as my mom turned around from where she was standing at the sink.

"Is that . . . is that the surprise?" I asked.

Mom smiled and pointed to the table.

"Why don't you go check?"

I ran over and Dominic glumly pushed the cage toward me.

"What is it?" I asked him.

"Dunno. It's, like, a gerbil or something," he said, shrugging.

Mom sat down in the chair next to Dominic. "It's a hamster, Mimi!"

I pushed my face against the white bars of the cage. In the corner was a caramel-colored hamster with dark-brown patches. His little black eyes darted around before settling on me. My breath caught in my throat—he couldn't be real! I leaned in closer, squinting, just to check if it was a prank. Only when I saw his tiny sides pulsing with nervous breaths could I finally exhale.

"For me? I really get to keep him?"

Mom smiled at me.

"Yes, you do! Happy Birthday, hon! You'll have to think of a name for him today while you're at Grandma's. We can put his cage over there in the window so he can look out while you're gone."

Dominic stood and loudly shoved his chair back in place. "Mimi gets everything," he grumbled.

"You got to wake me up this morning!" I cheerily reminded him, wiggling my eyebrows just long enough that he rolled his eyes in return.

Dominic had been in charge of waking me up every morning since he used my red alarm clock as the timer on the rocket he and his best friend Nigel built in the backyard. Mom decided this was the best way to punish Dominic until he saved enough allowance to buy me a new alarm clock, which I'd decided would be purple. I don't know if you know any thirteen-year-old boys, but take my word for it—they make terrible personal alarm clocks.

Mom, ignoring my furious eyebrow wiggling, stepped in. "Dominic, you get to see your friends at school, and Mimi doesn't get to—"

"Whatever," Dominic said, before stomping out of the room. Mom sighed and looked down at the tiles for a moment then looked up again with a smile.

"Grab your coat. We don't want to keep Grandma waiting."

Chapter Two

My mom played the Beach Boys in the car so I knew her good mood had returned despite Dominic's stomping. She whistled softly through her teeth as we drove.

"Maybe I'll call him Brownie!" I said.

"Sure, honey, that's a good name."

"But too ordinary, don't you think?"

"Well, I suppose there might be other hamsters who are nam—"

"Caramel? What about Caramel?"

"Now that's a nice—"

"Maybe I shouldn't name him after his fur color," I said,

reconsidering. "Don't judge a book by its cover. That's what Grandma says!"

"Well, maybe Grandma will have some ideas on what to name him."

The car wheels crunched to a stop on Grandma's gravel driveway, and with a quick kiss and another "Happy Birthday" from Mom, I swung open the door and shot through the front garden.

My grandma lives in a giant old house on a shady street lined with huge oak trees. My mom says Grandma has lived here ever since my dad was a little boy. My grandma spends most of her time in the big front room, and that's where I do my schoolwork and read to her. That's also where Grandma keeps most of her plants. She has thirty-nine in total in the house. My grandma passed the fifth grade a long time ago, and she can read to herself, too, but I heard her telling Mom that this way I can keep up with my education. Little does Grandma know, I've been up to some top-secret extra homework of my own.

"Grandma! You'll NEVER guess!" I threw my backpack down next to the front door.

"Is that the *eleven*-year-old?"

I heard her voice from the kitchen. She poked her head out into the hall with a big smile.

"Come on in, my Mimi-girl!" She vanished and then reappeared with a bouquet of sunflowers and waved it at me magician-style. "Your presence is commanded at a special birthday brunch! And then after, *yes*, YES, I'm sorry"—she waved away my expression as I opened my mouth to protest—"you need to finish your math booklet."

The extraordinary prospect of my very own birthday brunch trumped some extra-ordinary unfinished equations, and I skipped around the corner after her. Extraordinary: banana pancakes, whipped cream, and orange juice with pulp. Extra-ordinary: oatmeal-colored math booklets.

For an extremely extraordinary kid, I live a pretty ordinary life. That is, I used to live a pretty ordinary life. I used to go to a pretty ordinary school with old brown bricks and scratchy yellow chairs in the principal's office, with my extremely ordinary best friend, Patricia. And sure, I live in a pretty ordinary house, with a red front door and a brass knocker. But my pretty ordinary life completely changed almost two months ago. Because sometimes, an extra-ordinary thing needs to happen in an ordinary life for it to become extraordinary.

Extraordinary life or ordinary life, math still had to be done, and today I followed it up with spelling and then reading aloud. Most days followed the same pattern.

We usually took a morning recess before reading but only on days when the weather was nice. Grandma had refused to do yard duty for all of March. After lunch I would sit down to do either a music or art activity depending on the day. Grandma would cancel music on days when she had a headache, and I would have to save recorder practice for later. We took an afternoon recess to water the plants and Grandma would refill the bird feeder and make a cup of tea, and then we would end the afternoon with science or social studies. I preferred social studies, and I could tell Grandma did, too, because sometimes she would nod off during science.

My schoolwork today flew by, which was unexpected considering we were on a particularly dull unit in math, and Thursdays are the most boring days of the week. It's just a fact. It's surprising, too, because Thursday starts with a *T*, and the other day that starts with a *T* is Tuesday—a day that is entirely magical! It just goes to show that birthdays can make any day of the week magical. Especially a birthday that started with the greatest gift ever.

The big cuckoo clock struck three, and I gratefully dropped my pencil onto the table. Three o'clock is Grandma's nap time, and it's exactly one hour until Mom comes to pick me up after getting Dominic from his school. During nap time, I'm allowed to watch TV with subtitles on, so it can be quiet for Grandma to sleep, but recently I've been using the time to work on my secret research project. Grandma doesn't know the reason I only work on my project during her naps, so I've learned to stay in the living room until the snoring starts.

Today, though, I was restless as I sat beside her on the brown leather couch, still stuffed full of birthday brunch and math equations, with my mind racing and my hands drumming on my lap. I couldn't stop thinking about my hamster. I was so excited to have a brand-new best friend.

I had been best friendless for exactly forty-seven days—ever since Patricia betrayed me in the worst possible way. My new best friend options were slim because I didn't see the kids from school anymore, and Grandma sleeps far too much to be a proper best friend to me. Plus, when I told her that, she laughed in her huge bellowing grandma way that makes her earrings jingle, and I don't think I should have a best friend who laughs at me nearly as much as she does. I told her she

could be the first replacement, for when someone calls in sick. She seemed to find that just as funny.

After unsuccessfully trying to scratch under my cast for a few minutes, I stood up and began to softly pad around the room. The carpet cushioned my near tap-dancing feet. Why couldn't I think of a name?

Benjamin? No.

Bernard? Ugh.

Patricia! I smiled with glee at the thought but decided against it. Knowing Patricia, she would be thrilled.

I stopped and stretched, waiting for inspiration to strike.

Hands to the sky, wiggle your fingers. Hands to the floor. Hands to the sky, wiggle your fingers. Hands to the floor.

After more unsuccessful scratching and my third stretching rotation, I caught sight of one of the old pictures on the wall across from the couch. And it suddenly came to me: the perfect name! The very best one of all! I couldn't help but grin at my stroke of brilliance. As if by magic, Grandma's first snore rang out. I grabbed my pad of sticky notes off the coffee table, tiptoed up the stairs, and disappeared into the small bedroom on the left.

Sitting at the dinner table that night with Mom and Dominic, I cleared my throat and prepared for my big announcement. "I want to call him Harvey."

Mom looked up from her plate in surprise. Dominic turned red and fumbled a piece of lettuce off his fork. "Mimi!"

"What? That's what I want to call him. That's his name now."

Mom looked as if she was about to say something but then forced her mouth into a half smile and pushed her mashed potatoes around her plate. I had to admit part of me was enjoying their reaction.

"Mimi!" Dominic said, louder. "You can't do that, *dummy*."

"Dominic . . ." Mom warned.

"Why not?" I asked.

"Because—"

"Dominic!"

"Because that's *Dad's* name!"

Chapter Three

The crowd roared as Harvey Samuel MacNeil ran out into the blinding lights to take his bow. He stooped low as roses rained down on the stage then stood and lifted his arms above his head, waving at the adoring crowd. As he gazed into the audience, he could swear, for a moment, he saw a flash of a familiar freckled face. Just as quickly, the face vanished. He blinked. For a second, he'd seen his little girl. But no, it couldn't be!

The music swelled and the crowd began to chant ENCORE! ENCORE! He bowed a second time and took a deep breath, trying to clear his head. Harvey Samuel

MacNeil had to leave his family to achieve his extraordinary destiny, and Miriam Janine MacNeil had to be left. But an extra-ordinary event can be an opportunity for an extraordinary call to destiny. With any luck his daughter Mimi would realize hers soon. The audience continued chanting. He stood and faced the adoring crowd again.

When I was in the third grade, I met another girl named Mimi. We were in the same after-school art class on Wednesday nights. Because we were both Mimi, the class called her Mimi P. and me Mimi M. I thought it was easy to tell us apart because Mimi M. was extraordinary and Mimi P. liked to wipe her drippy nose on the front of her shirt.

My dad, on the other hand, was the only Harvey at his school. One of a kind. He never had to be Harvey M.! He was never mistaken for someone with a drippy nose, or cold hands, or unimaginative watercolors. He got to be Harvey! The only one! I used to think that if you had the same name as anyone else, it automatically made you less special. But now, I was changing my tune. See, it's one thing if you just happen to have the same name as someone else on the same attendance list, but it's a whole other thing to be *named after* someone extraordinary. That would be a great honor. I wouldn't know because I'm named after Great-Aunt Miriam, who's not only extra-ordinary but smells like celery and loves to fix my posture. But naming my new best friend wouldn't be like sharing a name with a kid at school or a smelly great-aunt namesake. I would give him the name of an inspiring role model!

That night before bed, I sat at my desk with my markers. I took the time to carefully curl the letters just right as I made a fancy name tag: *H A R V E Y*

He hopped around his cage, kicking little wood chips every-where as I carefully tied the name tag to the handle. I reached my finger in when I was done, and he pushed his nose against it softly.

Just like the human Harvey, hamster Harvey was one of a kind.

Mom was typing softly on her laptop at the kitchen table when I skipped in on Sunday night.

"Hi, Mama!"

Clickclickclickclick.

"Hi, hon."

Clickclickclicklclick.

"Mama?"

Clickclickclickclickclickclick.

"Mmhm?"

"I was thinking . . . Harvey has met you and Dominic, but he hasn't met Grandma." I paused as the clicking continued. "If Harvey is going to be a part of the family, like, you know, *really* part of the family, he should meet Grandma."

Clickclickclickclick.

Clickclickclickclick.

Clickclickclickclick.

"So, I wondered if it would be okay to take Harvey with me to Grandma's tomorrow?"

Mom's eyebrows drew together and the clicking paused.

"Mimi—"

"Because Grandma already said yes!" I continued. "So if you say yes then everyone has said yes, and I can tell Harvey it's a yes." I crossed my fingers behind my back. I needed Mom to let me bring Harvey to Grandma's. With any luck, tomorrow Harvey and I could both learn something from his namesake. After all, what are new best friends for, if not for helping with your secret research projects?

Mom sighed and tipped the screen down to look directly at me. The blue glow from her laptop screen made her face look more tired than usual.

"Sweetie, I'm sure Grandma is interested to meet Harvey, but I don't want him kicking wood chips all over, and your poor grandma having to clean—"

"He won't though, Mom. Honestly! I'll clean up and everything!"

Mom didn't look convinced. I had to admit, as a new family member, Harvey hadn't been the easiest to get used to—I'd learned over the weekend that besides running on his wheel, his favorite things included chewing on his cage bars, squeaking until midnight, and kicking wood chips out of his cage. But how could we expect Harvey to know manners if he had never been taught? All the more reason for Harvey to learn the ways of his role model sooner rather than later! And Harvey had to know as much as possible about his namesake if he was going to help me with my project.

"Grandma is so excited to meet him," I tried. "You should have heard her! She was asking me questions about him all day Friday."

Clickclickclickclickclickclickclickclick.

Mom scratched her jaw and then pursed her lips for a moment.

"All right. See if Dominic can help you load the cage in the car before he leaves for school in the morning."

I nodded and gave Mom a kiss on the cheek before dodging into the hallway for a quick victory dance. Harvey and I were off to Grandma's tomorrow for what was sure to be a secret project breakthrough. I tore up the stairs to tell him the good news.

On Monday morning after Mom dropped me off, I slowly

walked up to Grandma's house, balancing Harvey's cage in my arms and trying to ignore how the edge knocked against my cast. When I stepped inside, Grandma raised her eyebrows but said nothing. I did feel a little bad about lying to Mom, so I decided to tell Grandma the truth. Well, part of it.

"Harvey is helping with my research project!"

"Must be a pretty smart hamster!" Grandma remarked. She didn't ask too many questions about my project. I had told her it was for school, it was due at the end of the year, and, unlike some of my other schoolwork, I *really* wanted to work on it alone. That had seemed to settle it. Thankfully, Harvey's arrival hadn't upped her curiosity.

"Oh, he is!" I assured her.

A few hours later, when the cuckoo clock rang out, I tiptoed to the second floor, a brownie and my sticky notes balanced on Harvey's cage. At the top of the stairs, I turned left and stopped in front of a worn white bedroom door.

I glanced downstairs from under the banister. I could see Grandma lying on the couch, her feet sticking out from under a blue blanket.

Grandma had had her knitting circle over on the weekend, and if there was anything you could count on after knitting circle, it was a ton of leftover snacks and immediate snores the moment Grandma's head hit the couch cushions. Strangely, I had never seen any knitting around the house.

I glanced downstairs one last time, and satisfied that Grandma was fast asleep, I turned the knob and went inside.

My dad's old bedroom was painted a dark mossy-green. White curtains hung in front of a large window next to the bed. A light layer of dust lined the windowsill, which made me fairly confident that Grandma hadn't been in the room for a good long while. Yellow sticky notes covered two of the walls and thumbtacks held my evidence in place. A long piece of red yarn stretched across it all.

When Dad joined the circus, he signed a strict contract to keep information from the performer's family. My dad is so

extraordinary that if we were to know his exact whereabouts, the media would never leave us alone in trying to get all the details. Mom never talks about Dad at all because I know she doesn't want paparazzi following her to work. She's worried enough about business as it is.

Despite the contract, I did expect to hear from my dad more. But there was a lot about life on tour I didn't understand. I figured cell service was bad on the road, and with all the late-night performances, Dad was probably asleep when we were available to chat on the weekend and just starting his shows by the time we were sitting down for dinner together on weeknights. Not to mention the likelihood of phones being dropped from tightrope wires, melted by fire eaters, or swallowed by circus animals . . .

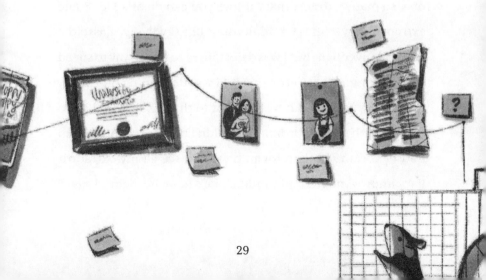

The truth was, I didn't really know why he hadn't been in touch. But maybe the secret project would help that become clear, too.

Little by little, over the past six weeks, I had collected information on my dad. Grandma hadn't seemed to notice the items I'd taken from around the house, and thanks to her naps she certainly didn't know I was spending that time in Dad's old room. To Grandma these were just Dad's childhood memories, but to me they were important clues to his extraordinary path. My dad was setting an example for me, and by studying the pieces of his extraordinary life, I would no doubt improve my own extraordinariness even further!

I was pretty grateful to have some help, though. As an already extraordinary person, I was a little stumped. There are only so many extraordinary things you can do as a kid. Some extraordinary stuff is for adults only, like skydiving, glassblowing, and silver hair. But I was determined to find a way to speed up my extraordinary growth, and I was depending on Harvey to help me figure out how to take it to the next level. I had to make myself so extraordinary I couldn't be ignored! And when Dad next came back to town, he would see all my extraordinary improvements and wouldn't dare leave me behind again.

Chapter Four

It was time for class to begin. I set Harvey's cage in the middle of the room to give him the best view.

"Gathered in front of you are the clues to my dad's extraordinary life," I began. "Exactly what made him so extraordinary? The people want to know. Can these details and clues be studied and learned? Can they help already extraordinary people become even more extraordinary?"

I grabbed an old fishing net I had found in the closet and marched over to the start of my red yarn timeline. I hit the first sticky note with a soft *thwack!*

Harvey Samuel MacNeil is born.

"Okay! So, here's what I have so far," I told Harvey. "On August 2, 1974, the most extraordinary summertime lightning storm ever was recorded. But it wasn't just any summer storm. It was the summer storm over Grimsby, Ontario, that welcomed my dad, Harvey Samuel MacNeil, to planet Earth. It was kind of like the Earth's drumroll or a bright, flashing, double-door entrance!

"Grandpa and Grandma weren't necessarily aware of the extraordinary significance of the storm," I explained. "I asked Grandma to describe it once, and she said that she doesn't remember the storm because she was busy. I don't get how she doesn't remember every single moment, but I prefer to put my own spin on it. Anyway!"

Thwack!

I snapped my net down on the next item, a few feet away. A faded picture of my dad as a little boy, outside of Grandma's old house in Grimsby.

"Dad had a seemingly ordinary childhood. He kept his talents secret for a long time. He did the same activities as the other kids at school. He played ball hockey, he went camping, he ate pizza on Friday nights, he wrote his spelling tests, and on his birthdays he begged for a puppy. The pizza continued but the puppy never happened."

I looked at the picture and frowned, considering.

"I do all of these extraordinary things! I eat pizza. I go camping. And everyone loves puppies!" Harvey gave a tiny sneeze, like someone opening a bottle of pop. "Oh, well, maybe not *you*, Harvey. And I guess I don't play ball hockey. But I mean— who *does*?"

Harvey sneezed again.

Oh, right. Dominic.

I lowered my fishing net.

"I'm sorry, Harvey."

This morning at breakfast, Dominic had refused to speak to me directly or even say hi to Harvey. On the whole, it didn't bother me too much since Dominic primarily communicated through noises these days anyway, but I had to say it was pretty rude not to greet a family member. When Dominic did refer to Harvey, he called him "IT." He even capitalized it. I know because he shoved a note under my door in the middle of the night that said, "Tell IT to stop running on the stupid wheel! I'm trying to sleep!!!" He even added a little doodle of Harvey running in his wheel with a big *X* through it.

Dominic is actually a really talented artist, but I would only tell him so if he used his powers for good, not evil. Plus, I never complain about the amount of noise Dominic and his best friend Niiiiigel make when they play sports in the driveway. I always say Nigel's name like that: *Niiiiigel.* It drives Dominic particularly nuts.

Even though Dominic's doodle impressed me, his attitude did not, and I made a mental note to add it to the extra-ordinary column later.

"Let's move on, shall we?" I tried to steer Harvey back on track. "When my dad was eight, Grandpa and Grandma packed up the whole house and moved from Grimsby, Ontario, right up to the big city of Toronto . . ."

I walked across the room until I reached a ribbon pinned to the wall.

Thwack!

"And it was in Toronto that his talents were first discovered. See, what he was really good at was swimming. Harvey Samuel MacNeil was such a good swimmer that he was practically part fish!" I looked at Harvey over my shoulder. "Check and check! I live in Toronto, a very extraordinary city, and I am a very, VERY talented swim—"

Another sneeze.

I narrowed my eyes at Harvey. He sneezed twice more and blinked at me before I was satisfied that he was done. I decided to forgive the offense.

"Moving on!"

Thwack! My net came down on a creased paper menu.

"My dad was really smart and got really good grades, so after he finished high school, they told him that he needed to keep going to school for years and years to come. School was really expensive, though, so he got a special swimming scholarship and a nighttime job at an extraordinary place called Hoppy Hoppy Brew & Pub. He was so good at that job, even though he was tired from spending all day at school, that they made him a manager."

I began to pace. Harvey followed me with his eyes.

"Now here's where it gets tricky. Hoppy Hoppy Brew & Pub closed down about seventeen years ago, and so far I haven't been able to find a managerial job anywhere. I offered to be Mom's manager instead of that brokerage lady she doesn't like, but she didn't follow up on the offer . . ."

Harvey had now climbed into his wheel for a nap. I cleared my throat loudly. I needed his help!

"For years all my dad did was swim and study and manage all

of the good Hoppy Hoppy people until he finished school and became a master."

Thwack! A diploma!

"Soon after that he met a very nice real estate agent, Mom, and they fell in love."

Thwack! A wedding picture!

I was trying to speed it up because my voice was hurting from all the throat clearing. Harvey still had one eye open. I started including some big hand gestures, like I had seen my teacher do, to try and keep his attention.

"The thing was, Dad was an extraordinary person living a totally ordinary life. He had a very nice ordinary wife, with a sometimes-nice ordinary son, and a totally extraordinary daughter. He drove every morning to his ordinary job at the college, and after work he went every night to the community center to swim before coming home to his ordinary house. But it just wasn't the same as his glory days. How could he be really, truly fulfilled with this ordinary existence?

"That's where Mr. Morelli's Big Top Circus Extravaganza comes in. The circus needed a talented swimmer for their newest act, a trick high dive, and when they heard of my dad's great talent, they knew they had to have him. So they brought the show to Toronto in order to recruit him, and they begged him to come with them on the road!

My throat got tighter. I cleared it again, but my voice grew higher pitched as I continued.

"Even though it was a tough decision, he couldn't look back. He knew what he must do. He got up one Friday morning, packed his suitcase, and left with the circus. Now he has to focus all of his attention on his new life and set an example for his extraordinary daughter."

Thwack! My school photo!

"He knew I could put the pieces together."

Harvey's one eye looked doubtful.

Thwack! My net hit the crumpled newspaper.

"He left me this clue to say goodbye. Don't you see, Harvey?" I clutched the net and took a deep breath before continuing. "It wasn't about fame or fortune. It was about living up to his extraordinary potential."

Harvey's eyes opened wide.

"It was about setting an example for me—and now for you, too. Wherever he is right now, I know that he's expecting me to learn his extraordinary ways and rise to my full potential!"

Thwack! The final sticky note. A question mark.

"Sometimes an extra-ordinary thing has to happen for people to become extraordinary."

I stared at the sticky note for a few moments before I remembered Harvey sitting there.

"Questions?"

He sneezed.

"Suggestions?"

He sneezed.

Harvey was right. We needed to find more clues.

EXTRA-ORDINARY	ORDINARY	EXTRAORDINARY
Dominic's doodles	Sleeping in class	Swimming scholarships

Chapter Five

"Grandma! Do you know what time it is?" I stood over the couch on Wednesday, my arms crossed. "It's way past your nap time!"

Grandma looked up from her book.

"You need your rest, Grandma! Doctors say elderly people need *lots* of sleep." I gave her my best expert look. It was ten past three and Grandma had decided to read today instead of taking her usual nap.

Grandma reached over and gave her coffee a stir as I threw my hands in the air.

I walked back and forth across the carpet impatiently. I had more work to get done! Dad had been gone for more than six weeks now. What if, as time passed, I became less extraordinary in his mind, and he didn't want to come home? I impatiently tugged on my belt loops as I marched.

Harvey had been banned from Grandma's on Monday after he was discovered chewing on a table coaster, while he had some time out of the cage to explore on his own. I had decided that today I would search the basement again for any clues I had missed, but how could I keep Grandma from getting suspicious?

I glanced her way. She happily hummed a little and took a sip of her coffee.

I sighed and sank onto the couch beside her, trying not to let my frustration show.

On the whole, I liked spending my days at Grandma's. For one thing, there's no way I would have had time to devote to my project if I still had to go to school. I did miss the smell of the pencil sharpener, getting to read aloud in reading groups, and playing at recess. But I certainly didn't miss playing with my ex-best friend. Patricia's games were never as creative as mine, and she was the silliest-looking runner I'd ever seen.

Actually, the only part of Cedardale Elementary that was remotely special was my teacher. Ms. Livi was short, but she had a big booming voice, and lovely lines around her eyes appeared when she smiled. Her eyes would nearly vanish whenever she laughed, and sometimes you could tell she was about to smile because the top part of her face would smile first. I thought it was pretty incredible that everyone else seemed to smile one way, but she went about it in reverse order.

Our classroom was colorful and busy, like the inside of a butterfly conservatory I visited once. There was always something to look at. Something moving, fluttering, or landing. Posters covered the walls, artwork coated the bulletin boards, and mobiles hung from the ceilings.

But butterflies or no, my classmates were completely ordinary and that fact alone made the whole classroom feel cocooned.

After the news broke at school about my dad joining the circus, Ms. Livi thought better of me attending an ordinary school. I remembered how satisfied I'd felt when I'd found out. The truth is, ordinary kids get jealous when you're born extraordinary. They probably don't want to be your friend because of it. I was glad I didn't have to worry about my classmates anymore. I imagined how big Ms. Livi's reverse smiles must have been when she went down the hall to talk to the principal, Mr. Miller. She even had him call my mom and ask us to come in . . .

The secretary's eyes flicked up to us as we walked into the office.

"Mrs. MacNeil? We've been expecting you." The secretary gestured to the open door behind her. "Go right on in."

I began to follow my mom, but the secretary held up her hand and gestured to the pale-yellow chair against the wall. "You can wait here, dear."

My mom adjusted her purse strap on her shoulder and gave me a half smile before walking into Mr. Miller's office.

I sat down and craned my neck to see through the opening. They shook hands over the desk as their voices wafted out.

"Mrs. MacNeil? I'm Bob Miller."

"Thank you for making the time."

"Please, have a seat!"

"Oh, thank you."

I heard some shuffling and the sound of a chair being pushed back.

"We wanted to check in on Mimi after what happened. We were concerned about her arm."

"Mmhm. I . . . well, thank you. The doctor said it was a compli-

cated break, so it'll take a while to heal, but she's doing much better."

"That's just wonderful to hear! She had us all worried . . ."

I shifted in my chair, the material scratching the back of my legs through my tights.

"Mrs. MacNeil, there's another matter we wanted to discuss."

"Oh?"

"Well, we know Mimi has had a tough few weeks . . ."

"It's been a difficult time. And Mimi . . . well, you know, she's a very sensitive child."

"Yes, of course. Mimi has mentioned her father has gone to—"

"Right. I—"

There was a crinkling sound and I looked up to see the secretary flipping through a magazine. It was one of those celebrity gossip magazines with all these pictures taken by paparazzi displayed with arrows and circled faces. I stared at the pages as she turned them in a flurry. The neon headlines jumped. The faces blurred. Suddenly the conversation in the office picked up.

"Not to worry—there's no need to explain," the principal said. "Now sometimes despite difficult times at home, a child can absolutely thrive! And we feel Mimi is one of those children."

"I understand."

"Her gifts are undeniable! We're feeling more and more as if *there's no need for Mimi to finish the fifth grade with us."*

"Oh. If you feel that would be best, I can—"

"She's way too far ahead! She would have no issue completing assignments at home and devoting herself full-time instead to her talents. Do you not agree?"

"Of course. I'll let her know."

"Please give her our best with this good news. Have a lovely day, Mrs. MacNeil, and congratulations to your gifted daughter!"

That meeting in the principal's office was how opportunity came calling. I sure wish opportunity didn't have such bad coffee breath, but bad breath or not, an extraordinary person knows that when opportunity knocks, you answer. I do wonder who Patricia has been playing with since I left. I was going to ask Dominic if he had seen her when he walked past the schoolyard, but then I remembered we're only on grunting terms these days. I absentmindedly began playing with the zipper on my hoodie, zipping it up slowly and then unzipping it in short spurts.

Ziiiiiiiiiiiiiiip.

Zip zip zip.

Ziiiiiiiiiiiiiiiip.

Zip zip zip.

"Sweetie, why don't you go and play something?" Grandma said, interrupting my thoughts. She was peering at me over her yellow mug and looking very pointedly at my hand poised on the zipper.

I stopped, ready to roll my eyes, when I got the most brilliant idea. I slapped on an extremely innocent smile and bounded to my feet to tower over Grandma once again.

"Grandma! That's a great idea!"

She picked up her book, seeming satisfied. I watched her closely as she flipped open to her bookmark.

"You know, I think I'll go and play *explorer*!"

Grandma looked back up.

When Dominic and I were little, we would visit Grandma each Sunday and play explorer. We would tie on bedsheet capes and roll up newspapers for binoculars, Grandma would pack us a picnic, and we would take it down to the basement and spend the rest of the day slowly going through all the old trunks or playing hide-and-seek behind boxes. I was way too old for it all now, plus it was obviously ridiculous. Explorers don't wear capes. But Grandma didn't know that.

She chuckled. "Ah! It's been a long time since I had my little explorers here. You go on an adventure and then you can tell your brother all about it tonight."

I gave Grandma an even bigger smile and gave her a thumbs-up as I headed swiftly for the basement door.

Chapter Six

Grandma's basement was a place of wonder—the kind of place I love, but it makes Mom purse her lips. The entire space was chock-full of stacks and stacks of bizarre items. There were towers of boxes full of everything you could imagine, and huge steamer trunks were filled with old-timey clothes, thick quilts, and trinkets like the ones you find at yard sales. There was a rock collection in the back, a broken pinball machine, and my personal favorite—an empty, cracked, tropical fish tank.

I know Mom thinks Grandma's basement has mice, and the truth is, I did see a mouse down there once, but I think my grandma wants to keep everything the same because all of

Grandpa's stuff is in the basement, too. I never met Grandpa, but I can tell from the basement that Grandma must miss him a lot. Mom and Dad were in Paris, on their honeymoon, when Grandpa died. I know because Grandma used to keep some of their pictures upstairs but moved them last month when Dominic and I came to stay for March Break. We stayed for two weeks instead of one because Mom was having an extra-or-dinary time of her own. I had checked the basement once during March Break while Grandma napped, but there had to be something I'd missed. Something that could replace the question mark at the end of my secret research project.

I turned slowly around before spying a large green trunk tucked under the stairs. Normally that trunk sat in the corner next to the tiny window, but it appeared to have been moved . . .

I slipped under the stairs and pushed my body against the trunk, shifting it out into the light with little shoves. The hinges squealed as I lifted the heavy lid. I breathed in the familiar musty trunk smell. Dust, mothballs, and the soft scent of freshly baked cookies. I think this must be what most grand-mas smell like.

I lifted a framed photo from the top and recognized it as

one that used to sit in the living room. Mom and Dad at a fancy dinner. Another picture showed them in front of the Eiffel Tower. The frames had gotten dustier since Grandma had packed them away. I softly wiped my sleeve over the glass. Mom and Dad smiled back at me. I tucked the familiar frames to the side of the trunk, pulled out a thick photo album that was sitting underneath, and flipped the cover open. The first picture was one I had never seen before—my parents standing in a train station. My dad must have been holding the camera from the way the picture was taken, and even though my mom had her hands up covering part of her face, I could tell she was laughing. They looked a lot younger. Dad was carrying a backpack and mom had a polka-dot T-shirt on and a sweater tied around her shoulders. He had his arm around her, pulling her in to face the camera. They looked happy. They looked like people in a story. I closed the album and dropped it back into the trunk as if it had burned my hands.

I reached further into the trunk and my hand brushed against something soft. My curiosity piqued, I pushed aside a few more photo albums and some of Dominic's and my baby stuff I had looked through in March to pull out a black wool hat I hadn't noticed before. It was one of those French berets people wear when they dress up as painters for Halloween. Was it my Dad's? Could it be another clue?

I turned and ran up the stairs and into the small bathroom off the kitchen. I pulled the beret on and looked at myself in the mirror. I was hoping I would look sophisticated, but I looked more like a sad black-and-white photo from a history textbook. Nevertheless, I was tingling with excitement.

I leapt into the living room. Grandma laughed when she saw me.

"Well! Who do we have here?"

"Please, sir! May I have some cheese and crackers?"

Grandma laughed harder.

"Sweetie, I'm not sure Oliver Twist wore a beret."

"Where is it from?" I asked, slipping it off my head and following her into the kitchen. She turned her back to me and took a moment to answer as she pulled out a cutting board and opened the fridge. She began to chop some cheese on the counter.

"It was your father's. He got it in Paris when he and your Mom were there."

Bingo.

"Oh wow! It's authentic!" Even the word tasted like adventure. "Why did he keep it?"

"Well, he used to tell these great stories about the street performers in Paris. He just loved them! Especially the mimes. He thought they were hilarious. He used to make your mom go out with him and watch them perform after dinner . . . He bought the hat one night then went back to the hotel and performed a routine for her. She said he was just awful at it, but they laughed and laughed. He was always so silly like that, your dad. He always had such a funny bone . . ."

Grandma trailed off as she spread some crackers out on a plate, her eyebrows furrowing. Poor Grandma must really miss Dad. I looked down at the hat in my hands. I knew how that felt. I popped the beret back on my head, leaving it askew. I widened my eyes and mouth into a silly surprised face and pretended to pound on an invisible wall in front of me. Then I mimicked silent crying with a big puppy-dog face. Grandma burst out laughing, her mood gone, and applauded.

"Well, Mimi-girl! You've got a gift! I better watch you closely or the circus will come scoop you up."

If you were to imagine an extraordinary moment of destiny, I bet you wouldn't imagine it in a kitchen on a particularly ordinary Wednesday. I bet you wouldn't imagine a plate of cheese and crackers or a replacement best friend—but this was my moment. Because when my dad left to be a trick high diver in Mr. Morelli's Big Top Circus Extravaganza one day in March, he left his ordinary life to achieve his extraordinary destiny. Grandma didn't realize she had just handed me the final clue. Of course! It was the key to my extraordinary life! I was my father's extraordinary daughter, trying to escape my totally ordinary world, and the circus was in my blood. He was just waiting for me to prove it.

Chapter Seven

The tent flaps flew open and Harvey Samuel MacNeil burst inside. He was frustrated. He walked over to the wooden bunk bed and gripped the end, tapping his foot absentmindedly against it as he thought. He knew Mr. Morelli would have a thing or two to say to him about his performance today. Six weeks on the road already and he still couldn't focus. The crowds loved him, but he wasn't fooling Mr. Morelli. His mind was somewhere else. Tomorrow the circus was headed off to their next stop and Harvey Samuel MacNeil would have limited time to master his next act.

To keep the crowds pouring in, Mr. Morelli had designed a new trick for the Extraordinary that was twice as daring. After only a few weeks of rehearsal, when the show opened again, the Extraordinary would climb to his high-dive platform, and this time he would dive through a ring of fire before landing in the pool of water below. As long as Harvey Samuel MacNeil could keep his mind on the dive and off the freckled phantom from the crowd, he was sure to be a success.

This would be his greatest challenge yet.

I skipped over to the front desk as we arrived at the library on Saturday morning. The librarian peered up at me over the top of his glasses.

"I'm looking for books on mime!"

"Mime?" he repeated.

"Yes! Mime. Or mimes. Wait, do they live in groups? Anyway, on the circus!"

He ignored my question. "Would you like to check the

children's section?"

I shifted my weight impatiently. "No. They need to be for *professionals*."

"Okay . . . well. Um . . ." He furrowed his brow as he scrolled on the computer. "Okay. It says here we have some instructional books. And there's also a videocassette! Do you have a way to play that at home?"

"Yes! My grandma has a VCR. Yes, please!"

He nodded and pushed his chair back. I followed his patterned knitted vest back into the stacks, hop-skipping with excitement.

Today was a *momentous occasion*. With the final clue in place, I had officially completed my secret research project. I had the answer I was looking for, the way to take my extraordinariness to the next level and prove to my dad that I, too, was ready to leave ordinary life behind. I had spent the last few days' worth of nap times packing away my project, and finally, I was ready for my next challenge.

It had been a quiet drive over this morning. Dominic grunted when Mom had asked him to come with us and continued to play his video game, not taking his eyes from the screen. But today I was feeling triumphant, and no one, not even Dominic, could have ruined my excitement.

Dominic had been generally grumpy for the past year, but that's because he was beginning to cross over. That's when you change from being a kid into a grown-up. Crossing-over doesn't happen all at once, though. From what I hear, it can take many, many years and it seems pretty painful. At least, it's painful to watch someone go through it! When you cross over, you get quiet and smelly and you only want to watch TV in the basement. That's one of the first signs. Dominic was only in *phase one*, and Dad always said it would get a lot worse before it got better. Back in February, I was beginning to suspect that my classmate Joel had entered phase one as well because he smelled extra bad after gym.

PHASE ONE

- Subject's vocabulary is reduced and early signs of silence set in.
- Subject communicates through grunts.
- Subject begins to smell and watch TV alone in the basement.
- Observed behavior: wall leaning and grunted contact established with other subject (Niiiiigel).

PHASE TWO

-Subject's vocabulary grows from grunting to include name-calling and frequently includes yelling and door-slamming.

-Subject experiences excessive sweating and explosive and random emotions.

PHASE THREE

-Vocabulary expands to include large words that are used as weapons against younger sister, who wouldn't know the large words.

-Subject exhibits eye-rolling and begins to use "adult voice."

-Subject shares knowing looks with nearby adults.

PHASE FOUR

-Subject achieves full adult status.

-Subject begins to show maturity and kindness is restored.

I figured that by phase four Dominic and I would be friends again. By my calculations, we only had 1,130 days to go! Things had seemed different for the past month and a half, though, and even worse since my birthday. For a little while it looked as though Dominic was going to graduate into phase two, but his attitude lately had really set him back.

The librarian walked in front of me and started rapidly pulling books off the shelves. He finally topped off the stack with a terrible-looking old video called "The Art of Mime" starring Marcel Marceau.

"I didn't know kids liked mime," he mused.

"Ordinary kids don't, I'm sure. But this is for research," I told him.

"Oh?"

"I'm putting on a mime show. I'm auditioning for the circus."

This was the first time I had spoken my new plan aloud. Silence followed as we continued our stare-off in the stacks, me peeking over the tower of books now in my arms.

"I see," he said, breaking the silence. Though this librarian wasn't the most interested and sympathetic audience, his eyebrows rose, and I was satisfied he seemed relatively impressed.

"Yes. Perhaps I'll advertise in the library!"

"Hmm."

"I'll need an audience. It's an important element of the performance, you know. To have an audience. Plus, I'm a relatively unknown and unappreciated artist, so advertising will be very important."

"Well . . . yes. I suppose so."

He looked unsure, but you can't expect everyone to know the ins and outs of the performing arts. I knew an interested customer when I saw one, though, and I made a mental note to return and sell tickets here later.

"Mimi!"

My mom stood at the end of the row of shelves. She beckoned to me.

"Ready to go, hon?"

As we checked out our books, I thought I saw her eyeing my selections. She didn't ask, and while my plan was still being hatched, I preferred it that way.

Chapter Eight

A mime is the highest breed of clown. Unlike regular clowns, mimes can't use words to tell a joke, so it's much more complicated to be a mime. Mime is all imagination, so it takes a very creative person.

There are seven distinct and important elements of a mime.

One, the beret. All mimes wear berets, but only truly extraordinary mimes have a beret right from Paris. Berets must be black or red.

Two, the face paint. All mimes must wear white face paint with black details. They have to draw either triangles or diamonds under their eyes. It's a hard decision.

It's truly the slides versus swings of face paint.

Three, a striped shirt or dress. All mimes must wear horizontal stripes, and they must be black and white!

Four, colorful shoes. That's only for the extra special mimes to wear, though.

Five, silence! All mimes need to stay silent when performing.

They can't even breathe loudly, even though they're performing very hard and despite the fact it has been a particularly smoggy spring, according to Mom.

Six, mimes wear special white gloves that draw the eye to the mime's hands. That's where the magic happens.

Seven, the mime needs a furry sidekick, but that's really only for extraordinary mimes. I know that ordinary mimes don't have them, but that's what would set me apart. With some luck and more careful allowance-saving, my furry sidekick would even have his own travel cage. Then he could travel in style to the circus.

The first thing you should know about rehearsing for a mime show is that no one will be interested in hearing about the seven distinct and important elements of a mime. In fact, gone are the days of respect for the high art of mime altogether.

Your grandma may refuse to drive you to the party supply store because the face paint you want still isn't on sale and her gardening gloves will serve just fine—don't mind the soil! When you ask to pick up some brightly colored presentation boards from the dollar store, she'll hand you a flattened raisin bran box from the recycling bin.

Your mother may insist that you use your words to ask to

be passed the salt at dinner because, given that your already-silent teenager brother is close to entering phase two of his crossing-over, mealtime is already mime-like enough anyway.

Said silent brother will insist you practice in the garage because he needs the living room for video games after school, and when you try to sweep out the garage for a stage, your hamster will kick wood chips into the area you just swept.

Most of all, though, your ex-best friend may see you practicing from her bedroom window across the street and find herself standing in the doorway of the garage to beg your forgiveness.

She won't say it in so many words, though.

"What are you doing?" Patricia asked.

"What?" I looked up, surprised.

"What are you doing?"

I didn't answer.

"Mimi?"

I picked a piece of soil off my glove to avoid making eye contact.

"Are you pretending to garden?"

I snapped to attention.

"What? No."

"Aren't those gardening gloves?" she pressed.

"No!"

"That's a weird sunhat . . ."

"It's not a—"

"I can help you garden. My Bubbe showed me how to garden!" Patricia is kind of like a hummingbird. She flutters so quickly she almost buzzes.

"No! I don't want to garden with you or Bubbe! I'm not gardening. I'm . . . I'm . . ." I was getting flustered. It was just like Patricia to not let someone ignore her.

"You're talking to me!"

"Yes! I mean . . . No!"

Patricia gasped and her hands flew to her mouth.

Patricia gets scared by everything. She's always making this silly surprised face and saying things like "Oh my! Spelling test! Oh my! Cinnamon on apple sauce! Oh my! A rainy day! Oh my!" Once I even saw her get surprised by her own shadow. She told me she had just never seen it that tall before.

"Oh my! Mimi! Do you have a mouse?"

I looked over my shoulder at Harvey's cage, and in one bound Patricia flew into the garage with her arms out.

"Oh my goodness!"

"It's a *hamster*! And anyway, his name is Harvey."

"Harvey? But Mimi—"

"If you want to hold Harvey, you have to be quiet," I told her. "He likes silent people best."

"Okay! Oh, please, Mimi. Let me hold him?" She switched to a whisper. "I'll be so quiet!"

"Fine," I snapped.

Patricia carefully opened the cage door and reached in with her dainty, pale Patricia hands. Her face broke into a huge smile as she pulled Harvey out. Patricia has this wobbly smile that looks like she's always about to cry, which makes sense because she's very delicate. My mom is always saying how gentle she is. *"Patricia is such a gentle girl!"* I don't think anyone has ever called me a gentle girl. All because I don't have lovely hands that play piano or a mother who peeks through the curtains, and I don't pick at my food or say "Oh my!" all the time.

"You're so lucky you got a hamster!"

I glared at her. "It was my birthday present. I told my mom I wanted a new best friend."

Patricia's eyes filled with tears and she softly put Harvey back into his cage. She sniffed and turned to go, but not before I caught a glimpse of her blotchy face. I felt instant regret. No matter what part she had played on that extra-ordinary day in March, she was just trying to be nice to Harvey, who was by all accounts very deserving of kindness despite his constant wood-chip-kicking.

"Wait! Okay, I'll tell you what I'm doing."

She clasped her hands together.

"Will you? Oh, please, Mimi, please!"

The sheer excitement on Patricia's face was even better than the satisfaction of speaking the plan aloud again. I basked in it for a moment longer.

"I'm rehearsing for a mime show," I finally told her.

"A mime show? Like . . . a clown show?"

"No! It's a *mime* show. Mimes are different than clowns. They're better!"

"Oh!" She looked shocked and delighted all at once.

"Yes." I tossed my head proudly and began to demonstrate my mimed lasso move. *Keep space in between the palms, stretch the rope out in front of you, hold one hand up high, and draw a circle in the air three times. Release! Pull the rope toward your body with one hand in front of the other.* Marcel would be proud.

Patricia's face lit up and she burst into applause.

"Oh, Mimi! It's so good! Will you teach me? I could be in the show—"

"No!" I dropped my invisible rope. "Mimes never reveal their secrets. That's why they don't talk!" I wasn't positive that was true, but it made sense to me.

Patricia's face fell. I felt a funny pang in my stomach.

"But . . ." I said. Her eyes flicked back up to me. "I guess I may as well let you join because you've already seen my top-secret rehearsal space."

She looked around. "The garage?"

I held up my hand. "Well, I have to share it with the car, but that's the perfect cover-up. No one would ever suspect I'm rehearsing in here."

She seemed to accept that explanation. "Okay, so who can I be for the show?" Patricia began to flap around the garage as she waited for my answer.

"Well," I ventured, adjusting my beret, "Harvey has been cast as my assistant, and it's important that he has a handler to take care of his needs when he's offstage. You can set up a dressing room for him and wait on the side with treats between my acts!"

Patricia looked like she was about to protest, so I quickly jumped in. "That's your final offer! You haven't been forgiven yet, so I can't promote you."

"Oh. Okay, Mimi." She offered another wobbly smile. I pointed to a lawn chair next to Harvey's cage. She took a seat and folded her hands in her lap, her smile faltering ever so slightly.

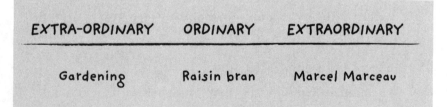

EXTRA-ORDINARY	ORDINARY	EXTRAORDINARY
Gardening	Raisin bran	Marcel Marceau

Chapter Nine

The best part about watching a mime video is there's no need for subtitles, so if your replacement best friend wants to nap in the living room, you don't have to worry about the volume keeping her up. My mime video and books led to more and more mime rehearsals as I began to develop my new skill.

Circus was in my blood thanks to my dad, so I took to mime quite easily. Because Harvey was my special assistant, he needed to be present at as many rehearsals as possible. This was kind of hard with the amount of time I spent rehearsing at Grandma's house, but when I came home each day I updated him on all the new skills I'd been working on.

As Harvey's new handler, Patricia was in charge of getting Harvey ready for rehearsals, so we developed a top-secret mime signal. Of course, the signal had to be silent. When I got home from Grandma's, I would go to my bedroom window, where I'd taped a piece of turquoise tissue paper, and through it would use a flashlight to direct a series of flashes at her window, which was her cue to meet me in the garage in five minutes. The thing was, it was difficult to see the signal in the daytime, so Patricia was usually at least fifteen minutes late.

We'd been rehearsing for about a week when Patricia hustled into the garage, late as usual, carrying a garbage bag full of props.

"Did you bring it?" I asked.

"Yes! It's here." She patted the bag and smiled proudly. "Oh my, Mimi! The finale! This is so exciting."

I took the bag from her. I was excited, too, but I tried to mask it a little. You know, for *professionalism*.

"This is the part we have to practice the hardest," I said. "It needs to look the very best of the whole show, so we have to start working on it early. It's a very important trick."

She nodded solemnly.

"I'll show you what I'm thinking."

I took a deep breath and launched into my dream finale trick, moving through the choreography in slow motion.

The mime signal was a good system, but it still didn't make Patricia trustworthy enough to know the real reason for my show. No one could know that—especially not Mom. She didn't think anyone knew the truth behind why Dad left home, and she certainly didn't know that Dad left clues for me. I knew I wasn't supposed to talk to Mom or Dominic about that. If he'd wanted to tell them, he would have left answers for them, too.

Extraordinary people are made for something more. That's why they can never stay.

Mom always knew Dad was made for something more. Well, she called it "something else." At least, that's what I heard her say on the phone with Aunt Daphne. But I knew she meant "more." Or else why did he leave his ordinary life? Maybe we were *too* ordinary. Except me. He knew I was special. But maybe he thought the rest of the family was just ordinary. Ordinary is okay, but I guess my dad was so extraordinary that Mom and Dominic seemed extra-ordinary to him.

I snapped out of my thoughts and looked up from my final pose.

"Something like that!" I said.

I took an experimental bow, and Patricia jumped up out of her lawn chair, clapping.

I lowered my prop and went to get a sip of water.

"It'll need a lot of rehearsal, I know—"

Patricia helped me slip the finale prop back into her bag as we discussed how it would look at the performance. I did want Patricia's input on the finale, though I'd made it clear that her help would not mean a promotion to director. Harvey sprayed wood chips across the garage floor as he hopped around his cage approvingly.

"So what do you think?" I asked. "For the final trick?"

Patricia grinned and held her arms over her head. "Encore!"

An extraordinary person doesn't waste time on ordinary thinking. I had to focus. I decided that two weeks would be enough time to rehearse for my show and that the performance would be on the second Tuesday of May. With my rehearsals well underway and my most important trick already choreographed, I turned my attention to the guest list.

I found Dominic digging a huge hole in the backyard garden. I approached slowly while he, completely oblivious, barely missed me with a large shovelful of dirt thrown over his shoulder. I noticed Nigel digging next to Dominic and I narrowed my eyes at him. He smirked at my approach.

"Hello, Dominic," I said.

"What, Mimi?" he responded dully, not looking up.

"Hello, Niiiiiiiiigge—"

"WHAT, Mimi? We're busy!" Dominic dug his shovel in.

"Why are you digging a hole?" I asked.

"It's a grave for your ugly rat," Nigel replied, snickering.

"Shut up! It's way too big for him anyway."

"Mimi! What do you need?" Dominic threw his shovel down and finally looked up at me.

"Well, I'm putting on a show. A . . . performance."

He crossed his arms.

"And, well, I need to make some invitations. But . . . um . . . I'm busy rehearsing and you're a better . . . You're good at drawing, and I thought maybe—"

"Are we invited to your baby show?" Nigel interrupted.

"NO!" I snapped.

"Mimi!" Dominic huffed. "We're busy, okay? Just make them yourself!"

I considered kicking dirt back into the hole as I turned to leave but calculated that between the two of them, hole or not, I wouldn't make it down the driveway without being caught. My stomach turned, and I felt for a moment like I was under-water. I walked away slowly to the sound of their laughter.

In the schoolyard at recess, some of the kids play this game called Octopus. It's kind of like tag, but if you get caught you become seaweed and can't play anymore. You stand in one spot, holding your arms out, and you sway. You let your body slowly drift and lean side to side like you're underwater. You can't do anything. You're just seaweed. You stand on the ocean floor and you sway.

On the extra-ordinary morning in March, I stood in the kitchen underwater, and I swayed. Mom said she had to go upstairs, and I just swayed. Dominic told me to pack my suitcase because Grandma was coming to get us, and I swayed. I swayed over to the sink, and I looked out the window at the empty driveway. I swayed over to the kitchen table and wrapped my slippery vine arms around the empty chair. I was just seaweed. Nothing to do but sway. And then I saw it. The newspaper lay open on the table.

SAYING GOODBYE TO THE BIG TOP.
MR. MORELLI'S BIG TOP CIRCUS EXTRAVAGANZA

I stopped swaying and tried to focus on the article in front of me.

"Set to leave Toronto and continue on its international tour! The show will close after a sold-out run of six weeks in the city. It boasts upcoming tour locations such as Berlin, London, and Barcelona."

My feet found solid ground and my slippery arms floated back down to my sides. I was back in the game.

You can't color with seaweed arms, so I did my best to push that memory out of my mind as I went up to my bedroom and sat down at my desk. I could hear Dominic and Nigel still digging in the backyard, but I opened my drawer of craft supplies and the sound soon faded away. The colors swirled in front of me as I began my creations, and I imagined the circus springing up from the page and coming alive right before my eyes.

I finished just before bed, walked into the living room, and threw down a stack of carefully drawn invitations made with construction paper and pastels. Mom raised her eyebrows but kept working. I wiped my stained hands on my jeans.

"I have to send these out," I said.

"All right, honey. Later this week we can—"

"Don't you want to know what they are?"

She finally glanced up.

"Well I fig—"

"They're invitations to my show!"

"I noticed you've been practicing something!"

I felt my cheeks grow hot. How much did she know? "Well, I can't tell you anything more because the rest is a surprise, but will you just . . . Can you mail them ASAP?"

Mom put down the paper she was reading and looked up at me.

"Hon, I've got showings all day tomorrow."

"Please, Mom? Please?"

She took my hands and chuckled as she turned them over gently, seeing the stains from the pastels. I gave her hands an urgent squeeze and she looked up at me again.

"All right, all right!" she groaned, teasing me.

"ASAP?"

"ASAP."

Chapter Ten

"MacNeil! Mail for you!" Harvey Samuel MacNeil looked down from the rehearsal platform to see the postman waving an envelope over his head at the entrance of the big top. From where he stood, the postman was no larger than an ant. He gave a wave in reply.

"I'm coming down!" he called.

He took a breath and then leapt forward into the air. His fingers closed around the first trapeze bar, and he swung up toward the bright stage lights. As he reached the very top, his stomach gave a flutter, and the bar changed direction, swinging back toward the platform.

On the second swing, he let go and let himself glide through the air for a moment before catching the next bar lower down.

The postman applauded as the Extraordinary swung from bar to bar through the tent before landing softly on the sand-covered floor. Even the high diver had to keep his other acts sharp. The postman dashed over and gave him a congratulatory slap on the back before handing him his mail. Harvey Samuel MacNeil accepted the envelope eagerly. He would have recognized the careful lettering anywhere.

"To Mr. Harvey Samuel MacNeil (the Extraordinary)"

He remembered when he had taught her that word, reading before bed one night many years ago. He closed his eyes and held the letter close to him. The memory nearly jumped off the page.

"Wait! Spell it again?"

"Mimi!"

"Please, Daddy? One more time!"

"E-X-T-R-A-O-R-D-I-N-A-R-Y."

"Wow!"

"Should I keep reading?"

"Yes! But wait, will you write it down for me, too?"

With shaking hands, he slid the envelope open and pulled out the invitation.

Now that my invitations were sent and I had Patricia and her wobbly smile helping to keep my assistant happy, my show was coming together. I had to admit that Patricia came in handy; Harvey wasn't able to clap, and we did have a slight issue with keeping him awake during rehearsals.

We'd decided on an old doll cruise boat for Harvey's dressing room, and after digging it out of Patricia's basement and washing the dust off the enormous toy with the garden hose, we set it up in my garage. I saw Patricia's mom, Trudy, watching through the curtains the whole time as we dragged it across the street. She probably still hadn't forgiven me for the time I convinced Patricia that we should ride the boat down the stairs in her house like a toboggan.

We dropped the cruise boat in front of the garage with a thud.

"From the top!" I declared.

Patricia wiped her face on her sleeve as she caught her breath.

"But Mimi, we already rehearsed the entrance a bunch of times."

"But we haven't rehearsed the entrance with the boat!" I countered. "Now that we have it, we need to try the entrance all over again to get used to it. It's an important set piece," I reminded her.

"Well . . . Okay, Mimi."

We took our posts at either end of the boat.

"Ready?" I asked.

"Yes!" She grinned.

Patricia gave an enthusiastic tongue-trill-drumroll as I put on my best announcer voice.

"Prrrresenttttttinngggggg!"

The drumroll stopped abruptly.

"Um, wait! Sorry, what's the signal?"

I looked up at her with my eyebrows raised. "The cue?"

"Yes! What's the cue?"

I sighed. "'Presenting!' Remember? Then we carry the boat in, and Harvey appears in a captain's hat, and—"

"Oh. Right! I remember now. Sorry."

"Fine. Okay! Ready?"

The drumroll began.

"Preeeeeesenting!"

I pulled on the one end, toward the garage, and she pulled on the other in the opposite direction. We didn't move.

"Patricia! What are you doing?"

"Wait, but . . . I thought you said that you push and I pull?"

"*I* pull, *you* push!"

"Oh. Sorry, Mimi."

Harvey, wearing an origami paper hat, watched us drag the cruise boat in and out of the garage three more times.

Patricia looked up and did a double take.

"Oh my, Mimi!"

"Patricia!" I dropped my end of the boat in frustration. "What now?"

"Harvey ate his hat!"

Rehearsal didn't end well.

I gave Patricia strict instructions to only return the next day if she had a replacement hat. She reminded me then that she couldn't come to rehearsal at all the next day because she had to help her mom with a special dinner. I wasn't impressed with the lack of loyalty from my hamster handler, and I told her so. Patricia was putting us behind schedule! Obviously she didn't understand how important the show was. She didn't know what was at stake. What if Dad came and we weren't ready? What if in his mind I was no longer extraordinary? What if he returned to the circus without me?

I spent the rest of the afternoon pulling bits of paper out of a tiny hamster mouth like he was a Pez dispenser.

With Patricia tears and Harvey drool all over my gloves, I went to bed in a foul mood and woke up the next morning with nervous thoughts jumping around in my head. The more nervous my thoughts, the more angry I got with Patricia. How dare she not come to rehearsal, especially after all the chaos she caused yesterday?

I felt a little bad watching her tiptoe out her front door with a tiny paper hat in her hands when I got home that afternoon, but I tried to push her out of my mind and instead focused on preparing my snack in the kitchen.

The show must go on. Well, maybe not today. But at least I could use the downtime to keep my skills sharp, I decided. And, having no other options, I knew who I would pick as my replacement helper for the day.

Harvey and I set up in the living room where Dominic was sitting on the couch playing video games. I walked pointedly over to the TV and stood in front of the screen.

"Congratulations! It's your lucky day!"

He tipped his head to the side to see past me.

I tipped my head to the same side to block his view.

"You've been invited to practice with a very talented performer, and rehearsal starts—*now!*" I mimed a birdie toss in the air and took an expert swing with my badminton racquet, sending it flying toward Dominic.

Dominic swatted, knocking the birdie to the ground.

He went back to his game. I picked up my downed birdie and retreated, preparing to regroup over my snack at the coffee table.

It's a very bizarre thing watching video games. Mostly it's just a lot of clicking of buttons and then the occasional swooping sound. It was a lot louder when Dad used to play. Then, there was a lot of yelling and laughter, but now there was just silence. I guessed Dominic must like silence because he still sat down to play his game every day after school like he had before the extra-ordinary day in March.

There was no point in asking him anything else because no, he didn't want any graham crackers, and no, he didn't want to say hi to Patricia, who was now waving through the living room window as she dropped the origami hat in our mailbox, and no, he definitely didn't want to play mime badminton on the back lawn. Though he did break his silence to point out that since he can beat me in normal badminton, why would mime badminton be any different?

I understood snubbing Patricia. She really doesn't understand how brothers are because she doesn't have one of her own, and frankly, I don't like the way she stares at mine, but the badminton comment I couldn't get past! I decided the only natural course of action was to play it in the living room, around and over top of Dominic, while he was playing video games and doing his best to pretend to ignore me.

Whenever the video game made a swooping sound, I responded with my own swooping sound as my invisible racquet made contact with an equally invisible, impossibly enormous birdie.

Swoop!

SWOOOOOOOOOP!

Swoop!

SWWWWWWWOOOOOOOOP!

Everything would have been fine if my opponent hadn't upped their game. Suddenly the swoops came fast and furious! Dominic glared at me as I began to dash around the room at top speed, swinging at flying birdies. I even rolled across the back of the couch to retrieve a particularly challenging shot for good measure.

As I dashed across the room at top speed, Mom walked in. She was holding a laundry basket in her arms and talking on her phone, which was tucked between her shoulder and her ear. Trying to dodge me, she tripped right over Dominic's second controller wire.

The phone dropped, the birdie dropped, and we all heard the three sad tones of Dominic's game ending as we began to untangle. Dominic and I, shamefaced, pulled our red-faced and flustered mom to her feet. All the while, Harvey kicked wood chips onto the carpet.

"Dominic! Why is this wire here?" Mom held up the second controller "Why do we need a second one?"

Maybe Dominic was tired of the badminton, or maybe he was upset the game had ended or ashamed of Mom falling, but he opened his mouth like he was finally going to say something before turning an odd shade of pink and snatching his second controller from her hands, yanking the wire out, and throwing it all the way into the kitchen.

Swoop!

Mom and I stood there shocked until he left the room. We heard the drumroll of him running up the stairs and the final cymbal crash of him slamming his door. Harvey kicked out a few more wood chips.

I let my racquet drop.

Chapter Eleven

I was midway through miming myself out of a box on Sunday morning when I heard a distinctly non-Dominic knock. Mom slowly opened my bedroom door and poked her head around the corner.

"Mimi? Can we talk for a minute?"

I dipped into an elaborate bow, gesturing toward my bed. *Welcome. Come in.*

Mom walked over and sat down.

"Honey, I couldn't help but notice when I was mailing your invitations . . ."

"Yes?"

Her fingers picked at the edge of the duvet.

"That . . . That you wrote one for your dad."

I froze. I focused on keeping my voice steady.

"Well, yeah! Of course!"

She looked at me for a moment before speaking slowly.

"Well, I mean, it's nice of you to invite him, and to think of him, but—"

I was growing frustrated. How could she look through my invitations without my permission?

"He's not just invited. He's the guest of honor!"

"He's—" She looked surprised.

"The show is for him, really," I blurted.

I ran my nails across the rough part of my cast like a xylophone while I waited for her to answer.

She spoke slowly. "Mimi, I need to—"

Suddenly words spilled out of me without control. "Maybe you're just jealous because he didn't let you know where he was going!"

"Mimi!" Mom looked at me, shocked.

"But *I* know. And this performance is for him! And he's going to come to it and he's going to love it!"

I couldn't admit to her that I would be leaving with him

afterward. Mom would find out soon enough. She cleared her throat.

"Mimi, I saw how you addressed the invitation and—"

"I can't talk anymore! I'm busy rehearsing for my show."

I sped out of my room, shutting my bedroom door behind me. How dare she think I wouldn't invite him? Dominic stood on the stairs in front of me, looking bewildered. He shook his head.

"Really, Mimi?"

My face burned in embarrassment.

"*Move*, Dominic!" My voice shook and I pushed past him.

He burst out laughing as I continued down the stairs.

Dominic's laughter pinged around my head like a mimed badminton rally as I ran through the house, out the back door, and on to the porch steps. A lump was rising in my throat. Tears poured out as I sat down and put my face in my hands. Suddenly, I was back at school on that extra-ordinary day in March, standing in my classroom.

They surrounded me, laughing, as I cowered in the middle.

"*She's such a liar!*" *Tara screeched.*

"*Yeah!*" *voices called out in agreement.*

"*Just tell the truth, Mimi! No one likes a liar!*" *Dylan Weisnowski said, snickering.*

"*You're just bragging!*" *Amna added.*

"*I can't believe she thinks that!*" *I heard one of the girls whisper behind me.*

More laughter.

I held the crumpled piece of newspaper in my sweaty hand. I desperately scanned the group and found Patricia, standing at the back, her face pale.

"*Tell them, Patricia! You know!*"

She shifted from foot to foot and looked down. "*Mimi, I'm sorry. Bubbe says I can't lie.*"

I pushed past the group, dropping my newspaper clipping, and ran down the stairs, grabbing the wooden railing beside me. I held it as I swung around the tight staircase corner. I tried to catch my breath, but I knew the tears were coming. The lump in my throat grew bigger and I heard the squeak of the large door opening at the top of the stairs on the third floor.

"*Mimi! Mimi, wait!*"

I looked up the winding staircase and saw Patricia's small, concerned face peeking down then flashing by against the ugly tile as she raced after me.

"Please!" she called.

Tears began to stream down my face as I jumped the last two stairs and pushed open the heavy double doors. The sudden brightness of the schoolyard blinded me, and I inhaled the fresh cold air, watching my breath escape in little puffs. I used the sleeve of my sweater to wipe at my eyes and nose, but as soon as I had wiped the tears away, more came to replace them. As I stared blankly into the blurry sunlight, I realized I had forgotten my coat. There was still snow on the ground, melting in dirty gray clumps along the fence. I walked slowly, shivering. It was weird to be alone in the yard. It felt like a ghost town. I squinted up at the window of my classroom on the third floor and saw a bunch of curious faces gathered there. Smiling, laughing.

I would show them.

The creak of a gate startled me out of the memory. Then I heard Patricia's tremulous voice.

"Mimi? Isn't it time for rehearsal? I brought cookies that Bubbe made."

Patricia sheepishly held out a container of cookies in one hand and a ziplock bag of extra origami hats in the other.

I wiped my sleeve across my face. The show must go on.

EXTRA-ORDINARY	ORDINARY	EXTRAORDINARY
Brothers	Bubbe's cookies	
Classmates		

Chapter Twelve

I stood up too quickly, and my body swayed like seaweed.

"Whoa, Mimi! Are you okay?" Patricia asked.

I grabbed the porch railing before I stumbled off the step.

"I'm . . . I'm not feeling very well," I started to tell her.

"Oh! I'm sorry, Mimi. Do you want one of Bubbe's cookies? Should I get you a glass of water? You should sit back down. Should we reschedule rehearsal?"

"No! We have to rehearse every day," I said firmly.

"The show is nine days away," Patricia replied brightly. "Aren't you so excited?"

In an attempt to make up for missing rehearsal the other

night, Patricia was being twice as enthusiastic, which only made me feel worse.

Patricia walked ahead of me, chattering, as we cut around the side of the house and headed to the garage. We came up to the small gate in between the houses and Patricia tucked the cookies under one arm, reached up to unlatch it, and walked through, still talking as she went.

I stood in place on the other side.

Why did Mom have to bring up the invitations? Didn't she know it was none of her business? And why did Dominic have to laugh at me like that?

Patricia turned around.

"Aren't you coming, Mimi?" she asked. "Mimi!" Patricia waved her arms at me.

The school doors flew open.

"Mimi, come back! We're going to get in trouble!"

Patricia stood in the doorway, out of breath. I ignored her and scanned the schoolyard. Then I saw it—one of the portables facing my classroom. It was perfect. I took off toward the squat building. I could feel them laughing. I could feel them staring.

"Let them stare," I grunted between clenched teeth.

I stopped out front of the portable, placing one hand on the porch railing. I looked back at the third-floor window.

Pointing.

More faces.

Good.

I jumped up onto the railing and turned my back to them.

"Mimi? Mimi! Don't you remember this part? It's the walking against the wind! And then the balloons, remember?"

Patricia was standing in front of me, holding a collection of painted cardboard balloons. I dimly remembered following her into the garage to start rehearsal.

"And after we can work on the finale! I brought the special prop again . . ."

I stared at her.

As hard as I tried to focus on the rehearsal, I couldn't shake the feeling of the extra-ordinary day. I couldn't shake the memory of what had happened. Mostly, I couldn't shake the image of Patricia's face staring up at me.

"Did you forget?" Patricia looked at me worriedly.

"No, I . . . I just want a break now, okay?"

I walked away from her and sat down in one of the folding

chairs in the corner of the garage. Patricia fluttered after me.

"Oh, okay. It's intermission now?" Patricia sat down near me and scooted her lawn chair over, scraping it across the cement floor as she spoke. "I wanted to talk to you anyway. Well . . . Well, um, Mimi, I've been thinking, and you know, I talked to Bubbe about it, and she thinks it's a great idea, too."

I was having trouble focusing.

"What is?" It was hard to get blown away by a strong wind, carried off by balloons, and then listen to your bumbling ex-best friend—all while trying to get your big brother's laughter and an extra-ordinary day out of your head.

"Well, I was thinking that, you know, I got an *A* on my last test—um, my math test, I mean—and maybe for the show I could, you know, sell the tickets!"

"Sell the tickets?"

My brain was ready to burst.

"Yeah! It could be, like, a favor to you because I know you don't even like math, and um, you didn't write the test or anything last week because, well, you know . . ."

A soft buzzing began in my ears, and suddenly I was back in the yellow scratchy chairs outside the principal's office.

"*Mrs. MacNeil, there's another matter we wanted to discuss.*"

"*Oh?*"

"*Well, we know Mimi has had a tough few weeks . . .*"

"*It's been a difficult time. And Mimi—well, you know, she's a very sensitive child.*"

"*Yes, of course. Mimi has mentioned her father has gone to—*"

"*Right. I—*"

I covered my ears, trying to block out their words. Their actual words. But the memory played on.

"*Mrs. MacNeil, we are concerned by Mimi's behavior of late.*"

"*I understand.*"

"*We would suggest—rather, we would insist—that Mimi take some time away from school.*"

"*Oh. If you feel that would be best, I can—*"

"*We feel strongly that this is what's best. We've had other parents from the class express some concerns as well, and I'm sure you agree Mimi's health, and the health and safety of our other students, is what is most important.*"

"*Yes. Of course.*"

"*Let's see how these next few months go. We can touch base and meet again soon. I'll have our guidance counselor join us and—*"

"JUST STOP!"

I waited for the buzzing to die down.

"Wha—?" Patricia stared at me, surprised.

"STOP!" I repeated. "No, you can't sell the tickets, and no, I don't want to hear anything else about it! I'm so tired of everyone laughing, or trying to change my idea, or—"

I covered my face, but I could feel the tears starting to fall again.

"Rehearsal is DONE!" I yelled.

I grabbed Harvey's cage. Digging my fingers in between the white bars, I ran back into the house and all the way up to my room, slamming the door. I put Harvey's cage under the window before going over to my desk, pulling out a piece of construction paper and grabbing the closest marker.

"GO AWAY" I scrawled across the page. I took out the roll of tape from the top drawer and slapped a long piece across the top. I flung my bedroom door back open, letting the doorknob smack against the wall with a satisfying crack before pushing the sign down hard on the white wood. I shut the door with a crash for good measure.

Harvey kicked excitedly now that we were back upstairs, and I went over to kneel in front of him. I pulled him out of his cage, letting my tears fall as I held him against my face, nuzzling into his fur.

"I hate . . ." I didn't even know what.

"I hate everything right now," I whispered to him. He sneezed in reply. I went over to my desk and sat down, putting Harvey on my lap. I stroked his nose with one finger as he looked up at me.

"What do I do?"

Harvey blinked. He blinked again. Then he sneezed again.

"You're right."

What did it matter if they didn't understand? I wasn't going to be here much longer. After the show I would be leaving with Dad and Harvey, and we wouldn't be coming back.

I took out my construction paper once more and I cut out three identical squares. Then I took out my red marker and wrote across the top of each:

UN-INVITATION.

Chapter Thirteen

With the opening only three days away, and with it his daring new trick, Harvey Samuel MacNeil was rehearsing harder and harder. He dashed offstage and behind a tent curtain to grab a sip of water. He bent over, trying to catch his breath, as the jugglers took the stage for their act. Next to him, on the other side of the curtain, a crisp voice cut through the air.

"Where did he come from anyway?"

"Toronto, apparently! Calls himself the 'Extraordinary'! He came on the road all alone, poor man."

His heart dropped. He heard a mocking laugh.

"To think he can barely manage the high dive as it is, but diving through that flaming hoop? It takes a professional!"

"Well, it's no wonder. I hear he's miserable after leaving home. You can't possibly perform a trick like that if your heart's not in it . . ."

The voices grew more and more distant until they disappeared altogether. Harvey Samuel MacNeil stood behind the curtain with his heart thumping. They were right. The circus wasn't what he imagined. He had only ever dreamed of the good parts and the high points. The crowds cheering, his final bow, the smiles. But after the show, when the other performers were greeted by their friends and family, he stood alone, off to the side. The acrobats and sword swallowers and even Mr. Morelli himself had found their homes on the road—and he had left his home to come on the road. He reached into his pocket and closed his hand around the folded piece of construction paper.

At Grandma's house the next day, I decided nap time would best be used as a nap for me, too, since I had stayed up way past my bedtime finishing my un-invitations. I had woken up early that morning to make my deliveries, taping one to Dominic's video game controller, one to Patricia's screen door, and the last one to Mom's silky work blouse. She'd know I really meant it, too, because it's pretty hard to tape things to silky work blouses.

Grandma and I both lay down in the living room with the couch pillows under our heads. I woke up to Grandma gently shaking my shoulder just before Mom was to arrive.

"Mimi-girl!" she whispered. "Are you ready for your surprise?"

Considering the extra-ordinary nature of yesterday, I was absolutely ready for a surprise. I hopped up with lightning speed.

"Okay! Close your eyes!" Grandma ducked into the next room and called over her shoulder, "Keep them closed! Keeeeeeep them closed!"

I waited, eyes closed and ready.

"Open!"

In one hand, Grandma held up a black-and-white striped

long-sleeved T-shirt under a black overall dress. In the other was a pair of white gloves.

It was the perfect mime costume.

"The face paint is waiting for you in the bathroom, and . . ." My eyes filled with tears, and I flung myself around Grandma's waist. She patted my back.

"There, there, Mimareema! What's wrong?"

I spoke into her sweater.

"Thank you, Grandma. I'm sorry that you're only a replacement best friend. Because really, you and Harvey are the only friends I've got right now."

"Well, now, I don't mind! Grandmas aren't supposed to be best friends, and I'm sure you'll work things out with Patricia soon. But if you'll let me, how about I be your Fairy Grandmother, hmm?" She cupped my face with her hands.

Grandma's eyes were green like mine. Green like Dad's.

"I'll miss you, Grandma."

"You'll miss me?" She looked confused but put her arm around me for one last squeeze before letting go. "We've still got some time before you head home for dinner!"

I took my new costume into the bathroom to get dressed, and then Grandma helped me powder my face white, leaving

my eyebrows and mouth uncovered. She drew black diamonds under my eyes, like mime tears, and two big dollops of red on each cheek before applying red lipstick to my lips. I put on the beret and pulled the stretchy black-and-white material over my neon-green cast. I looked in the mirror.

It was hard to recognize the mime staring back at me. She looked young and happy and devotedly silent. No sign of a broken arm. She didn't miss school one bit! She had no need for friends because she had her trusty hamster sidekick, Harvey, and a very extraordinary dad who'd soon be showing her the ropes in her new circus job.

I was ready.

Chapter Fourteen

"Mr. Morelli! Mr. Morelli!"

His boss flipped open the tent door and disappeared into his office. Harvey Samuel MacNeil was no follower, but in this case, he ran in after him. Mr. Morelli looked up as his prized performer burst in, crossed over to his desk, and threw down a construction-paper invitation.

"Mr. Morelli, please, I need a leave of absence!"

"A leave of absence? Days before our opening night?" Mr. Morelli boomed. "You must be joking!" He threw his hands in the air.

"Please, Mr. Morelli, you don't understand—I need to go."

Mr. Morelli picked up the invitation on his desk and looked it over.

"Mime show?" he mused. "This mime, this 'Extraordinary,' what's so special about her?"

"She's my daughter, sir."

The ringmaster put the invitation down and paced around the room for a moment, considering.

"We'll make it back in time, and she'll perform with me on opening night. You have my word!"

Mr. Morelli surveyed him with a stern look.

"Two extraordinary MacNeils, hmm?" He broke into a grin. "Why didn't you say so!" Mr. Morelli grabbed him by the shoulders. "Go and get her!"

Harvey Samuel MacNeil couldn't believe his good fortune.

"Thank you, sir! You won't regret this."

"Yes! Yes! Don't be late for her show. Off you go!"

The second rule of Extraordinaryism is extraordinary people can never doubt they're made for extraordinary things. Even when extra-ordinary happenings occur, they must never be held back by doubt. Or in my case, by un-invited audience members.

The day of the show finally arrived after an exhausting week of rehearsals in the garage with Harvey. The cereal boxes I had been saving had become a rather large mountain by the side door, and I had to get them painted and posted in time for show day. Luckily, with the red paint stirred and ready, the messages were on the tip of my brush: a "Mime show this way!" for the telephone pole down the street, a "NO ORDINARY PEOPLE ALLOWED! for the garage door two houses down, several red arrows looping around the block and directing people to the garage, and most importantly, a "Harvey and the Extraordinary" over the garage door.

I stood back and admired my work. Without Patricia to help, I hadn't had time to advertise my show, no one had sold tickets, and I was twenty-three dollars short of a new travel cage for Harvey. But as I stood and gazed at my last sign, the sunlight bouncing off the duct tape holding it up, my bright future felt like the only thing that mattered.

I put out a selection of lawn chairs facing the garage for the audience members. I walked my favorite one, a floral purple, to the back and set it up on its own between the aisles. After considering it for a few minutes more, I painted an additional "GUEST OF HONOR" sign and taped it to the chair.

"Best seat in the house!" I told Harvey over my shoulder. He whirled his wheel in reply. I looked at the chair again and turned my head, examining each angle.

"Doesn't look very cozy, though, does it?"

I threw open the door to the house and skipped into the living room. I selected my prey and, like a crocodile, clamped my arms around the medium-sized armchair and dragged it toward the garage. I took me three tries to squeeze the chair through the door, which included pushing from the house side, hopping over it, and pulling from the garage side, and even jumping in the middle and wiggling the chair back and forth from within. With a high-pitched wailing sound from the doorframe, I finally squeezed the chair through and dragged it to the back to replace the floral one. I then covered it in birthday-party streamers and added the Guest of Honor sign, though it took me a while to stick them in place. Like silky work blouses, it's hard to tape things to velvety armchairs.

"Now *that* is the best seat in the house," I told Harvey, who had fallen asleep amid these antics. Nocturnal best friends are like that.

Harvey's seat wasn't too bad, either. Without Patricia to watch him in his dressing room, I placed his cage in an old red wagon that I had found during another exploration of Grandma's basement. The wagon wheels were squeaky, but I figured out if I played circus music while I wheeled it in, the noise didn't seem so bad. I had to practice the entrance several times to master the play and pause sequences of my new system.

I was lucky that Patricia had left all of the props in the garage, so my grand finale could still happen, but without her help I had to get even more creative with some sections of the show. For one, I had dragged in Dominic's skateboard ramp from the backyard and was using it as a platform. I could walk the edge like a tightrope, and when standing on the tall side, it felt like a proper circus high platform. It gave me a pretty big thrill to stick my toes over the edge and balance. I had also smuggled home evidence from my secret research project in a shoebox and worked it into the show. Dad was going to love that!

With the garage all set up, I went upstairs and packed a suitcase for myself and Harvey then hid it in the hydrangea bush behind the house. If Mom heard me bumping down the stairs with it, she didn't let on.

I took a seat in the floral lawn chair, all ready to go, by five thirty. The show was set to start at exactly seven o'clock. Grandma, my hair and makeup crew, was to arrive by six, and then she would stay in the house and have dinner with my uninvited guests until showtime.

The plan was in motion.

Chapter Fifteen

Fields sped by in flashes of green outside his window. Harvey Samuel MacNeil drove at top speed. Today was the day, and he couldn't miss it. On his dashboard sat the open invitation.

Harvey Samuel MacNeil had packed in a rush, but he had left enough time to take his hard-earned money and buy some special fabric, which he couriered to his mother. He needed his extraordinary girl to look the part when he brought her back to the circus. He had sworn his mother to secrecy, and all would be revealed upon his arrival. He parked the car quickly—he had just one last stop to make.

Harvey Samuel MacNeil dashed into the shop and threw his wallet down on the counter. The store clerk turned around.

"Yes, sir, can I help you?"

He gave his order without hesitation.

"A dozen red roses, please!"

The clerk nodded and began to prepare the bouquet. Harvey Samuel MacNeil could hardly contain his smile. Wouldn't she be so thrilled to see him? The store clerk pulled out wrapping paper and the Extraordinary held up his hand.

"No wrapping, please! I need to be able to throw them onto the stage!"

The clerk smiled.

"Ah, very good, sir. For a performance?"

"Yes. For a performance."

One thing you don't consider when you issue multiple un-invitations is that you might not have as many audience members as you originally planned on. Specifically, with five minutes until show time, only Grandma stood lined up outside the garage. While trying to ignore the gray head frequently poking in, I had draped a sign around my neck that read "USHER."

"The house is not yet open, ma'am!" I kept reminding her.

Luckily, I had a full house of patrons waiting in my bedroom. I raced inside to grab them. I placed a stuffed animal on each chair, leaving one seat open in the front row for Grandma and of course reserving the chair for the guest of honor at the back. I looked over my work with satisfaction. The smiling faces stared back at me, black beady eyes focused and ready to watch the show. I took a bow and they continued smiling.

I cleared my throat and hollered loud enough to be heard in the house. "See, Dominic? We sold out! Who's laughing now?"

Grandma poked her head around the corner again, and this time the usher let her in.

"The house is open, ma'am. Please take your seat!"

With an eyebrow raised at my other patrons, she made a beeline for the guest of honor's chair.

"No, ma'am, I'm afraid that chair is reserved. Your seat is up here!" I gestured to the front row. She once again raised an eyebrow but came to the front of the garage.

I had never performed my full show for an audience. Patricia was supposed to attend my mandatory dress rehearsal, as I had stipulated in the contract I made her sign, but I had ripped up the contract and shoved it through her mail slot after delivering her un-invitation. Even with a whole roll of tape holding it together, I didn't think it would stand up in court.

"Wow! Front row!" I remarked, trying to sweeten the deal as Grandma sat down. She blinked at me but gave a little smile.

"Now!" I said, putting on my stage voice while eyeing the open garage door. "The show is about to begin. We're just waiting on one final patron, our guest of honor."

Grandma looked confused and glanced over her shoulder. She raised a hand.

"Uh, Miss Mimi?"

"My name is the Extraordinary, audience member!" I continued in my booming stage voice. "And questions come later in the show!"

"Well, quickly, I just wanted to remind you that, um, your mother—or, your manager—says that the show has to be done for seven thirty."

"Yes! Yes, indeed!" I boomed. "My manager has made this clear, and I'm using a special system to keep the show moving along!"

I pointed to the egg timer, sitting on a milk crate, that Mom made me promise to use. If you ask me, making up rules for the show after being un-invited was pretty rude, but the manager controls the post-show snacks, so I figured it was best to go along with it.

Now that I looked at the timer, though, I realized a few minutes had already passed. And I had a lot of show to get through.

"Well then, I suppose we'll just get started slowly," I said. "I'm sure we can catch the guest of honor up after."

"Oh!" Grandma's hand shot up again "The Extraordinary? I forgot to mention there's been a surprise delivery for you. From an *admirer!*"

I tapped my foot impatiently and dropped my stage voice.

"Grandma, you mean a FAN!"

"YES! Of course, a *fan*." She pointed to the other side of the garage.

I looked over, and hidden behind a watering can, on a storage shelf, was a bouquet of red roses. I gasped. I ran to the garage door and stuck my head out, looking up and down the street. I just knew they were from Dad.

How tricky of him to send them before he arrived!

"Okay!" I announced to the street. "I guess I'll start the show since no one else is coming!" I winked at Grandma. She looked blankly back at me.

I prepared my entrance with Harvey, wheeling the wagon into the back corner of the garage. I ran over, clicked play on play on Mom's old mp3 player, took a deep breath, and ran back to my wagon. I dramatically wheeled it in, leading with one trembling jazz hand in the air. I made it to center stage, dashed off to pause the music , and dashed back to center.

"Welcome to Harvey and the Extraordinary: A MIME SHOW! This is Harvey, and my name is—"

I glanced up midsentence and my eyes landed on the empty armchair.

"Um." I stopped. I glanced nervously at Grandma. "Um, sorry. I forgot my line. I just . . . I'll start again, okay?" I tugged at my sleeve impatiently. "The beginning was way better in rehearsal."

Grandma nodded encouragingly and made little queen claps with her hands as I reset.

Dash to hit play, jazz hand out, wagon in! Dash to hit pause.

"Welcome to Harvey and the Extraordinary: A MIME SHOW! This is Harvey, and my name is THE EXTRAORDINARY! I'm not famous yet, but I will be soon."

I glanced up at the empty chair again.

I didn't understand. If this was a trick he was playing, it had gone on too long. I shook my head to clear my thoughts. I needed to focus. *The show must go on!*

"Our guest of honor isn't here yet, but he'll be joining us very soon. Thank you for coming! Did you find the garage okay?"

Grandma nodded.

"Did you see my signs?"

Grandma nodded again.

"They're made out of cereal boxes."

More queen claps.

"On with the show!"

I strode over to a flip chart I had taken from Dad's old office. Using a piece of broken trellis as my pointer, I tapped on each element of the show in turn.

"First, I'll be performing my puppet show, 'An Extraordinary Birth.' Then I will perform my mime specialties—getting out of the box, walking against a strong wind, and being carried off by balloons. I'll end with my *extraordinary* grand finale!"

I glanced back at the chair again. Still empty.

I fixed my hat before starting the puppet show. I climbed behind the skateboard ramp and used it to block my body. I pulled out the evidence from my research project. I had carefully hot-glued a popsicle stick to each piece of evidence to create my puppets. The popsicle sticks were numbered so I could remember the order without hesitation. I grabbed the first one and began.

"On August 2, 1974, there was recorded in history the most extraordinary summertime lightning storm ever. It wasn't just any summer storm, though. It was the summer storm over

Grimsby, Ontario, that welcomed Harvey Samuel MacNeil to planet Earth!"

I moved popsicle stick along the edge of the ramp. I peeked over to see that Grandma, now wide-eyed, had moved to the edge of her chair. The art of suspense! I commended myself on such an *effective storytelling method*. I continued on, pulling out my picture-of-Dad puppet, and wiggled it across the ramp as I spoke.

"Harvey Samuel MacNeil had a seemingly ordinary child-hood. He kept his talents a secret for a long time. He did the same activities that a lot of other kids at the school did! He played ball hockey, he went camping, he ate pizza on Friday nights, he wrote his spelling tests, and on his birthdays, he begged for a puppy. The pizza continued but the puppy never happened. What he was really good at, though, was swimming. Harvey Samuel MacNeil was such a good swimmer that he was practically part fish!"

I pulled out my first-place ribbon puppet and let it swim across the edge of the ramp. Now Grandma had started to look worriedly toward the guest of honor chair. Even she noticed how late he was running!

I was just nearing the part where Dad joined the circus when the sound of a car horn split the air.

Chapter Sixteen

He circled the block desperately, hands spinning on the wheel as he rounded the corner. Cars lined the street; driveways were full! He had finally made it home only to find nowhere to park the car. He glanced at the dashboard clock. Seven fifteen on the nose. Already fifteen minutes late? What would she think of him? She would think he wasn't coming. He searched desperately for some kind of sign he could send her. With nothing left to lose, Harvey Samuel MacNeil leaned on the car horn as hard as he could.

I'm coming, Mimi! he thought. I'm coming!

I stopped in surprise and then turned to peer out the garage door. He must be here! But—

Nothing.

I couldn't see him, but I knew he was nearby. If I timed it right, he would make it just in time to see my grand finale, the most impressive part.

I rushed through my mime sequences, barely taking time for my expressive faces or to acknowledge the nervous queen claps coming from the front row. The egg timer ticked along in anticipation of his arrival. Finally, I placed my cardboard balloons down after an expert, moon-worthy landing of my mimed flight sequence.

"And now! Ladies and— *Lady* and creatures of the audience. The moment you've all been waiting for!"

I ran to the side of the stage, threw open the garbage bag on the floor, and pulled out the secret finale prop—a golden hula hoop. I held it over my head solemnly.

"For her final act, the pièce de résistance, she will be performing the famed trick of her extraordinary father! Assistant? If you please?"

I wheeled Harvey's wagon next to the ramp and used it to prop the hoop up.

"The high dive through a flaming hoop!"

I ran up the skateboard ramp and stood on the highest edge.

The ramp was barely a few feet off the ground, but I was hoping it still looked impressive.

"The Extraordinary's final act!"

I wiggled my feet forward and let my toes peek over the edge. The timer counted down. Any second, he would walk through the door and at that moment I would leap into the air. I extended my arms out to the sides, poised for takeoff.

Tick tick tick tick tick tick.

I stared at the door and paused on my perch, ready to jump. My breath came faster and faster as the timer ticked on.

Tickticktickticktick.

I squeezed my eyes shut just for a second, and with a jolt I was back in the schoolyard on the extra-ordinary day in March.

The portable was cold and icy under my palms. If I extended my hands fully, I could just reach the top. With a deep breath I jumped from the railing, throwing my body against the side of the portable and pulling myself up, the way I'd climb onto a dock at summer camp. I heard a shriek from across the yard. I had almost forgotten that Patricia was standing there watching me. I wriggled onto the top of the portable, resting on all fours as I got my bearings. The roof was frozen, dirty, and cold. I moved slowly, crawling into the middle, and then toward the edge closest to the school.

"What are you doing? MIMI!" Patricia's voice wobbled and cracked. "MIMI, GET DOWN!"

With shaking knees, I put one foot in front of me and slowly rose to a crouch. I looked up at the classroom window, where even more kids had gathered. I could see mouths moving and wild pointing.

"P-please!"

I ignored her.

The school doors clanged shut with a dull metallic sound. I glanced over, and Patricia was gone.

As I slowly stood up, my stomach dropped. I was up pretty high. Higher than I thought. The wind pushed against me. I tried to focus, but the cold was creeping in through my thin sweater. Down on the ground in front of the porch was a dirty snowbank just close enough for me to jump into. I measured it with my mind—imagining pushing off the portable, leaping over the porch and into the snowbank below.

I cleared my throat.

"Ladies and gentlemen! Children of Cedardale Elementary! Right this way!" I held my arms above my head in V for victory.

The smiles in the window disappeared.

"She's fearless like her father, heir to the high-diving throne!"

The eyes in the window widened. "The one—"

The pointing began again, this time frantic. "The only—"

I squeezed my eyes shut as I choked out my final words. I bent my knees, ready to spring. "THE EXTRAORDINARY!"

I heard the crash of the school doors and my eyes flew open as Patricia tore across the schoolyard with Ms. Livi and the principal.

"MIMIIIII!!!!"

I shot straight up in surprise, knocking myself off balance. I stepped back, but my foot skidded across a patch of ice and suddenly I pitched forward.

For a moment, I was underwater, swaying like seaweed. I was in the kitchen swaying like seaweed. I was in the air swaying like seaweed.

And then I was on the ground.

Patricia wailed. Then nothing.

DING.

The timer went off.

Chapter Seventeen

The third rule of Extraordinaryism is that all ordinary people must be forgotten. Ordinary people must be left behind.

I looked around the garage in shock.

"He didn't come."

Grandma looked panicked. She stood up.

"Mimi . . ."

"I can't believe he didn't even—"

"Mimi, sweetie. He's not . . ."

I still stood on the ramp, but I didn't know how long I had been there. A day? A year? Everything felt frozen but my mind was racing. I knew Grandma was watching me, but I couldn't bring myself to say anything to her.

I guess he didn't want to meet Harvey. He probably didn't want to meet him because he knew Harvey was ordinary. Ordinary like me.

My brain fought back and forth, wanting so badly to be wrong.

He's just parking the car!

He didn't come.

Maybe he forgot the way?

He didn't come.

He ran out of gas!

He didn't come.

He would have called if he couldn't make it.

He didn't come.

Maybe the circus couldn't give him the day off!

"There is no circus." That one I said aloud.

"No," Grandma answered softly.

"He just left."

"Yes."

I lay face down on my bed as I listened to Mom and Grandma's murmurs in the kitchen. I wasn't sure how much time passed before there was a soft knock on my bedroom door.

"Mimi?" Grandma slowly opened the door. Her shadow appeared on the wall in the lamplight. "Can I come in?"

I didn't move. She tried again.

"Mimi? Please."

I sat up and wiped my eyes.

"Did I smudge my diamonds?" I asked her.

She didn't answer. She reached over and took my hands and waited.

I took a deep breath.

"I . . . I didn't mean to lie. I just . . . really, really wanted it to be true!"

Grandma brushed a piece of hair out of my eyes.

"Mimi, sometimes we make up stories because they seem easier than what we have to face. Sometimes stories make the difficult parts of life exciting—or just livable! But in the end, Mimsicle, the stories aren't real." She gave my hands a squeeze.

"But without my story, I'm just going to be sad," I gulped out between sobs.

"Honey, it's okay to be sad. But just because he isn't with the circus, it doesn't mean he didn't love you. And it doesn't mean you can't still love him!"

I thought about that as my tears continued to fall, and then like a cruel reminder, the timer rang out again in my mind.

Tick. Tick. Tick. DING.

"Someone who leaves with no good reason isn't extraordinary," I said. "And no one who gets left behind could possibly be extraordinary."

I lay back down on my bed.

Grandma was silent for a moment. Then she spoke quietly.

"I know it may feel that way now, but that feeling will pass. You'll see."

I so badly wished Grandma would leave me alone. I so, so badly wanted to rewind and go back to yesterday because the truth was that I loved my story. I wanted it to be true. The roaring crowds, the spinning technicolor, and the heaping bags of popcorn under the big top. But Dad wasn't waiting for me. There was no fame, no swinging trapeze, and no high dive through the flaming hoop. There was no hand to hold as I took my bow, no grand adventure waiting, and, worst of all, no promise of seeing Dad again. With every word she spoke I saw my perfect story, and my perfect life, moving further and further away until it was so far off it wasn't even a dream.

I felt so stupid. The kids at school were right.

My tears said enough. After Grandma slowly got up and left my room, she passed my Mom, who was coming up the stairs. They spoke softly, and then Mom came to the doorway.

She put on her bright face and waded over to my bed, picking up discarded costume pieces as she went.

"You know, Mimi, I was awfully sad to have missed your show." She kept her eyes on my costume as she folded it against her body before placing it at the foot of my bed. "Grandma said it was wonderful. If you'll let me, another day I'd love to see it . . . and I'd . . ." Her voice faltered. "Well, I'd love to be your guest of hon—"

I cut her off.

"Could you please call Mr. Miller? Tell him I'm going back to school tomorrow morning."

I turned over to face the wall. I lay there until I heard my mom's footsteps disappear down the stairs. When I was sure she was gone, I got up slowly.

Through my tears I closed my door. Then I knelt in front of the chart and used a marker to update it.

EXTRA-ORDINARY	ORDINARY	EXTRAORDINARY
Bucket hats	Pumpkins	Ruffley umbrellas
Turnips	Irish dancing	Zebras
Falling asleep in movies	Principal Miller's coffee breath	Hawaiian pizza
Orange (color)	Back crawl	Orange (fruit)
Video games	Mom	Art class
Non-chocolate milk	Dominic	Orange (soda)
Raisins	Putting on sunscreen	~~Dad~~
Skateboarding ramps	Cheesecake	Painted toenails
Aunt Daphne's kisses	White chocolate	Turquoise
Dominic's doodles	Sleeping in class	Swimming scholarships
Gardening	Raisin bran	Marcel Marceau
Brothers	Bubbe's cookies	Hamster blinks
Classmates	Ticket sellers	
Laughter	Mimi	
	Harvey	

Chapter Eighteen

The first rule of Ordinaryism is that ordinary kids go to school.

Maybe some rules are meant to be broken, but they're not first rules. They're first for a reason. And kids who go to school aren't supposed to break rules. If you break them, they may ask you to stay home until you're willing to not break rules or until your mom assures your principal you seem more consistent and "Yes! *Stable!*" in your behavior when he repeatedly asks.

When Grandma called me on the phone to check in this morning, I told her that even though I heard Mom use the word, I wasn't sure if it was true. And then Grandma said she thought my principal was an absolute moron anyway. I had never heard Grandma use that word, but it sounded true to me.

Upon their triumphant return to school after a very dramatic and—some people might say—tasteless scene, followed by a leave of absence, an extraordinary kid might have put some thought into a cool, back-to-school look. But I went with my favorite overalls instead, and comfy or not, overalls don't really say triumphant.

In fact, I was feeling pretty far from triumphant. I was feeling silly and small, and most assuredly ordinary. I wore a long-sleeved shirt to cover most of my cast because I didn't want the other kids gawking any more than I knew they already would.

I supposed that after scarfing down some toast and packing their backpack, an extraordinary pet owner would feed their pet themselves, but Dominic was already down the front walk and I had run out of time, so I called out for Mom to do it as I left the house. I crossed my fingers she heard me over the shower.

Ordinary kids go to ordinary schools. They walk there with their ordinary brothers, who drop them off, and when they get there, they sit with their ordinary best friends. That last rule I made an exception for, though, because Patricia was still my ex-best friend.

Cedardale Elementary was a completely ordinary place. The floors were speckled, the ceilings were speckled, the lights flickered, and the PA crackled. Inside the school, despite any attempts at heating or air conditioning, it was cold in the winter and hot in the summer. All the classroom doors were painted a sickening bluish-green that reminded you of the dentist's office. The gymnasium was lined wall to wall with felt banners of past athletic victories and the bells rang before school, after school, twice at each recess, and twice at lunch.

The teachers and students at Cedardale Elementary were completely ordinary, too. It was exactly where I belonged.

When I walked into my classroom that morning, the room felt silent and uncomfortable. I could tell Ms. Livi was trying to put everyone at ease because she was reverse smiling more widely than normal and waving her arms even more as she spoke. My desk sat in the same spot—the left side of the second row next to the sink. At first, it almost felt as if the world had paused, as if I had been abducted by aliens and no time had passed at all. My pencil was still sharp, and it was tucked into one of my notebooks where I had it last. But kids kept shifting their eyes to look at me then looking straight ahead when I looked back. On the extra-ordinary day in March, these kids were laughing at me. But no one was laughing now.

I guess being feared was better than being teased.

The morning went by in a blur, and my feeling that no time had passed quickly faded, replaced by painful reminders that I had been gone. The book I had never read that the rest of class was partway through in group circle. The projects lining the walls that I didn't recognize. My "Mimi" magnet, which was pushed off to the side of our magnetized "Class Tasks" list. No matter how many tests or oatmeal-colored work packets I had written at Grandma's, I had missed out.

When the bell rang and everyone headed downstairs to the lunchroom, I began to get nervous. Where would I sit? Certainly not with Patricia. But was I ready to ignore her if it meant eating alone in front of the whole class? When it came time to pick tables, however, Sadie and a few other girls from the class called out to me.

"Mimi! You can sit here!"

They moved down on the bench, and I gratefully jumped at the chance. Sadie was pretty nice as far as ordinary friends go, and her mom always smiled at me.

"Thanks!"

The second rule of Ordinaryism is that ordinary people eat lunch with their ordinary friends.

We chewed in silence for a while, and then I looked around, startled. I realized I had no idea where Patricia was. Sadie caught my eye as I scanned the lunchroom.

"She doesn't eat here anymore."

"Huh?"

"Patricia! After you . . . left, she started going home for lunch. Her Bubbe picks her up."

"Oh."

I tried to appear casual about the news, but it made me a little sad to think of all the girls eating together, and Patricia sitting with Bubbe.

I was grateful Sadie and the others girls solved my lunch-room problem for the day, but I had to admit they had very little imagination. I usually found their games boring. They didn't laugh a lot, and when they did, they giggled politely.

Sometimes when Patricia laughed, I could get milk to come out of her nose.

Walking back into the classroom that afternoon, I found a blue-raspberry push-up lollipop on my desk. Blue raspberry is my favorite flavor because it's extremely rare and inventive, and there was only one person at school who knew that. Then I remembered—extraordinary flavors are only for extraordinary people. I was ordinary now. I brushed it off the side of my desk and sat down quickly. Out of the corner of my eye, I saw Patricia cringe as the push-up lollipop hit the ground before burying her head in her textbook.

As the afternoon passed, I found myself glancing across the row of desks more and more. In the days at Grandma's house, whenever I thought of Patricia, I imagined that she was happy at school without me. I imagined she didn't miss me at all. I imagined her at lunch, surrounded by the other girls and giggling politely with them. I imagined them working on their group projects and picking out all the boring push-up lollipop flavors like cherry and green apple. But here she was, eating lunches at home with Bubbe, and here I was with a blue-raspberry push-up lollipop between my sneakers.

On the day two summers ago when I convinced Patricia to ride in the doll cruise boat down the stairs into her kitchen, something profound happened. It was profound how we scratched the walls on both sides the entire way down. It was profound how we landed in the kitchen smack in the middle of Patricia's mom's book club just as she was serving the coffee cake. But the most profound thing of all was that after we hit the first landing and not so gracefully rounded the corner, we took flight.

I expected an "Oh my!" I expected a wobbly yelp or a cry for Bubbe. But instead, Patricia opened her mouth and unleashed what can only be described as a scream of absolute freedom.

A top-of-the-roller-coaster, won-the-lottery, raining-candy kind of scream. An open-mouthed, full-voiced battle cry of pure joy. I can't confidently say what shocked the book club more. All I know is that after we landed, the book club spoke as a collective chorus:

"*Oh my!*"

Making sure Patricia wasn't looking, I bent down, picked up the push-up lollipop, and slid it into my desk.

When Dominic and I got home from school, I went right into the kitchen to make myself a snack. I cut up an apple and smeared it with peanut butter. I would always add a few extra spoonfuls when Mom wasn't home.

I'd dragged the velvet armchair back into its usual spot, and Dominic had his second controller plugged in and strung across the living room the way he liked it best. Today I balanced my snack in my hands and stepped slowly over the wire one foot at a time. I reached over to move the controller so I could sit down, and Dominic shot his arm up toward me.

"Don't touch it, Mimi!"

I looked over in surprise.

"Don't touch it!" he repeated. "It's—" He seemed like he was going to say something else but changed his mind and stared back down at his lap.

"It's not yours, so just don't touch it, okay?"

I stood there and looked at Dominic as he went back to his game.

I don't often look at Dominic.

For one thing, if you stare too long, he starts to turn pink and then he'll yell at you. But today I stopped and really looked. Dominic looked far away. He looked sad. He hadn't been leaning against walls as much as he used to, and he spent most of his free time playing his game. He hadn't even been drawing anymore, and that was his favorite thing.

I looked at the second controller sitting there in the empty armchair, and I finally realized something. Dominic was waiting for him, too.

I put my snack down on the coffee table in front of him.

"You know you can have some if you want."

"Nah. Already ate," he mumbled back.

"Dominic?"

No answer.

"Dominic?"

"Yeah?"

"Can I play?"

He looked up.

"Can I play your game with you? It looks fun, and . . . It looks like you're supposed to have a second player."

He met my eyes then. He didn't say anything, but he nodded slowly and pointed to the chair.

It took me a while to get the game. Dominic patiently demonstrated how to jump and which button to press to go in which direction. He even occasionally pointed at the screen and mumbled "Good!" but mostly it was a lot of swoop. He was being pretty encouraging, though, so I made a mental note to bump him up to phase three on his crossing-over chart.

I glanced over at my brother and thought I could see the tiniest hint of a smile.

"Mimi! Dinner!"

"One second!" I called. Two hours of swooping had me starving, and I quickly pulled Harvey's bowl out of the dish rack to make him his dinner before sitting down for mine. I ran over to the window seat and stopped. I realized guiltily that Harvey's cage was still in the garage. After the show last night, I had forgotten to move him. Poor Harvey, sitting alone in the garage and probably feeling all forgotten! My eyes stung with the memory.

I slipped through the garage door, chatting to him as I balanced his bowl.

"Harvey, I'm sorry! I know you've been waiting out here for me—"

I looked at the wagon sitting on the far side of the garage and found myself staring at an empty cage of woodchips and an open door.

Chapter Nineteen

The third rule of Ordinaryism is that ordinary people can become extra-ordinary at any moment.

I stood out on the front lawn as the sun set. I was breathing deeply, trying to stay calm. My stomach was doing flip-flops. I shut my eyes tight. I could hear Mom in the house calling out to Dominic to grab flashlights. I shivered, realizing I hadn't grabbed a sweater. As if in a trance, I had just walked outside.

We had checked the whole house, top to bottom. The chances of Harvey going back into the house when the garage door was wide open were slim. Mom insisted we check the house first, though, and it became clearer and clearer as we searched that he was nowhere to be found.

I'd looked for him in the garden while Dominic swept the backyard and Mom called Grandma.

Now I stood waiting on the lawn.

Mom came out the front door carrying sweaters for each of us, and Dominic followed with the flashlights. I tried to hold back my tears as Mom slipped the sweater over my shoulders and put her arm around me.

"What we need is a good plan! Flashlights on, everyone. Dominic and I will take one side of the street, and when Grandma gets here, she and Mimi will take the other."

At that moment, I saw a frantic Grandma driving down the street toward us.

"Not to worry, Mimi-girl! The rescuers are here!" she called, as she parked and stepped out of the car. Mom and Grandma exchanged looks when Mom handed her a flashlight. I waited silently to get started on the search.

My head was spinning.

How could Harvey leave me? Why did everyone keep leaving? How extra-ordinary do you have to be for only bad things to happen to you?

Grandma and I crossed the street and began to look for

Harvey. As the evening got darker and darker, I could see Mom and Dominic's flashlight beams swinging around, and as they swung, neighbors wandered out. Their voices swirled around me.

"Is everything okay?" Ms. Perez peeked out from her front porch two doors down.

"Oh! Poor Mimi! Well, we'll keep our eyes peeled all right!"

"Well, now, let me come and help you check our garden!" Mr. Warner called from across the street.

"How about out front in the trash there? Would he try to get some food out of the bin?"

I felt a terrible tightening in my stomach as I listened to my mom's replies. What if Harvey was hiding in one of the garbage bins? If the truck came along and emptied them, how would he ever find his way back home again?

Grandma seemed to read my mind. She put her hand on my shoulder.

"We'll check every single one. We'll find him, Mimi!" she whispered.

But I wasn't so sure that Harvey wanted to be found. Not by me.

Curtains flipped open and curious eyes peered out as

screen doors slammed and people stepped onto their porches to watch us search. The adults chatted in soft but concerned voices.

"Well, isn't that too bad!"

"Good luck, Mimi!"

"Don't you worry . . ."

"How about we put up some posters?"

Most neighbors looked hopeful, but some raised their eyebrows in doubt. The truth was, I felt the same way. Between the raccoons, cats, and garbage trucks, the chances of me ever seeing Harvey again were slim. When I saw it on their faces, I felt it even more inside, and the tears starting coming.

We eventually swapped sides of the street and worked our way back toward the house. When we got there, I sat down on the doorstep with my head in my hands.

"S-should we try to look around the block?" I stammered. Mom and Grandma exchanged looks before Grandma softly answered.

"Mimi, I'm not sure a little hamster could make it all that way. I think we should stop our search for now and pick it up again in the daylight."

I started to argue, but Mom quickly spoke up. "Mimi,

why don't you stay home from school tomorrow? You and Grandma can keep searching, and you know what?" She lowered her voice. "Maybe it was too soon to go back to school anyway, honey! It seems like—"

"WE CAN'T GIVE UP! WE CAN'T GIVE UP ON HIM!" I yelled.

Even if Harvey hadn't wanted to leave, I'd let him down.

My outburst seemed to make Dominic nervous. He wandered back over to the front garden with his flashlight, making clicking sounds with his tongue while he searched. Mom, Grandma, and I stayed on the doorstep while I cried.

"He's going to think that I left him," I managed to get out between sobs. "I was so worried about my show that he'll think I forgot about him, and I . . . I didn't! He'll think he was never important to me! He'll think he's so ordinary that I left him, but he's so, so extraordinary."

I let the crying overtake me, and Mom wrapped her arm around my shoulders.

"Oh, honey." I felt her shake and realized she was crying, too.

We sat there for what felt like forever, and then I heard a tiny throat clearing.

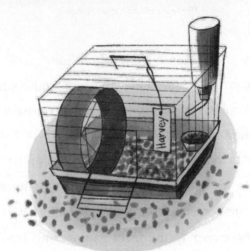

Chapter Twenty

Patricia stood in front of us, dressed in an enormous fleece sweater pulled over top of what I knew to be footie pajamas tucked into paisley rain boots. She looked pale and wide-eyed, and she was absolutely covered in mud. She stood with a flashlight tucked under one arm and her hands clasped tightly.

"Oh, hi, Patricia," my mom said, as I tried to wipe my tears away. "Sorry, sweetie, we're just finishing up our search for the night."

Patricia held her clasped hands out in front of her and fluttered over.

Unfurling her fingers, she slipped a soft, warm clump of

squeaking fur into my lap. I gasped.

"HARVEY!"

I held him against my cheek as I sobbed into his fur. He responded by wiggling and squeaking. Dominic rushed over as Mom and Grandma stood up.

"Oh, Patricia, we can't thank you enough!" Mom said.

"Mimi's been so worried! Oh my goodness, how wonderful!" Grandma chimed in.

"Honey, we can't tell you how grateful we are."

I wiped my face on my sleeve and spoke up. "H-how did you find him?"

"Well . . ." Patricia blushed. "I was lying in bed and I kept seeing all these lights in my window, and I got up because I thought that maybe you were doing the secret mime signal, Mimi! It seemed like a funny time for a rehearsal, but I got up anyway . . . and then I saw a bunch of people with flashlights out on the street, and I could hear some of the neighbors talking, and then I thought—oh my! And I realized what must have happened! And then, well—I snuck out."

Patricia wrung her hands. Mom raised her eyebrows and said nothing, while Grandma tried to hide her smile.

I was rightfully astounded.

"You snuck out?"

Patricia squared her shoulders and repeated it again, dropping to a half whisper partway through. "I snuck *out*. I went to the backyard and began to search, and sure enough I found him in Bubbe's vegetable garden! He was pretty quick, but I got him!"

I did a full head-to-toe scan of Patricia. Her face was covered with smudges, leaves stuck to her fleece sweater like burrs, and the knees of her pajamas were dirty. She shivered. I looked down, feeling guilty.

"Thank you," I whispered.

She looked back at me, not blinking.

"That's what true friends do."

After we helped the fugitive safely sneak back into her house, we celebrated with a round of hot chocolate at the kitchen table. Harvey got fresh wood chips and an extra-large helping of dinner. We called goodnight to Grandma as she headed back out to her car, and I chased her down the front walkway for one more hug. As I came back in the house, I heard dishes clinking in the kitchen and Mom humming as she loaded the dishwasher.

I shifted in the doorway, watching her for a few moments before going in.

"Mom?"

She turned around and held her arms open as I walked over. She wrapped her arms around me, and I closed my eyes as we hugged. I could feel her cheek resting on the top of my head. She sighed.

"I miss him too, honey."

We stood like that for a while.

"I love you," I whispered.

As I left the kitchen to head up to bed, I stopped in the hallway and peeked into the living room. Dominic was crouched by the window seat petting Harvey. If he'd heard me and Mom talking, he didn't let on. I watched as he slipped two extra treats into Harvey's bowl.

When I got to school the next morning, I didn't have time to talk to Patricia before we all sat down at our desks. I spent the morning organizing and reorganizing in my mind what I was going to say. Would she even accept my apology? The truth was, I was dreading having to talk about it. Two months was a long time to be mad, and even though part of me was impressed I had managed to keep it going so long, mostly I was ashamed.

Patricia was dressed extra ridiculously today in floral-patterned tights, a polka-dot dress, her paisley rain boots, and just in case the sun came out, her tie-dyed bucket hat that she had made three summers ago at day camp. Somehow her appearance made the idea of apologizing all the more embarrassing.

At morning recess, my chance finally came. I carried my lunch bag outside to eat my snack on a picnic bench. I settled at the table and bit into my apple, scanning the yard for Patricia. But before I could find her, my gaze landed on the portable, and I was transported back to my final moments at school in March.

"Mimi! Mimi!"

The faces leaning over me were hazy and glowed softly red, then blue, then red again. I could make out Patricia, who was standing closer than the rest. She reached out and pushed something into my hand, and pain shot through my body. Red. I must have cried out because she backed away, white as a sheet. I saw tears spilling down her face. Blue.

"I'm so sorry, Mimi! It's all my fault!"

Ms. Livi had her arm around Patricia and was trying to comfort her. Then Mr. Miller came into focus.

"You did the right thing coming to us."

Patricia held her head in her hands.

"No! No! I made her fall."

Ms. Livi hugged Patricia as I heard the crackle of a walkie-talkie and felt myself being lifted. The ambulance doors closed. I could barely feel my hand now. But when I looked down, I saw that it held the crumpled piece of newspaper.

A loud shriek interrupted my thoughts.

I shot to my feet. Dylan Weisnowski was dragging Patricia by her braids across the schoolyard. He pulled her around in a circle a few times before he came to a stop and slapped them against her back like reins.

"Giddyup!" he yelled.

"Let me go!" Patricia shrieked.

"Why, you gonna tell on me? Let's go, horsey!"

Patricia resisted and Dylan pulled the braids tight again. He had her pinned, like a paper butterfly to a Cedardale bulletin board.

With no teachers in sight, I reached into my lunch bag and unsheathed my weapon. I wouldn't let Dylan get away with this. I ran across the yard brandishing my yogurt tube like a knight preparing to joust.

"Let. Her. Go." I spoke through clenched teeth and narrowed my eyes at Dylan.

He snorted.

"Or what, Mimi?"

I swung my yogurt tube in a series of fast flicks while coming closer. He held up his hands.

"Okay, fine! It's not even worth it. Jeez!"

He walked away, and Patricia put her hands to the back of her head, slowly unbraiding her hair. She looked up at me shyly.

"Thanks, Mimi."

I took a deep breath. It was my moment. Time for the speech.

My mind went absolutely blank.

Patricia blinked.

I sighed. And then—

"That's what true friends do."

She answered with a huge smile, and we walked back to the picnic bench.

"Mimi?"

"Yeah?"

"I hope your yogurt didn't get warm."

After school was over, Patricia and I walked home together. Dominic stayed late to work on an art project, so we didn't have to worry about speaking in code. It turned out not talking to your best friend for two months leaves you with quite a lot to say. I told Patricia all about spending my days at Grandma's house and my secret research project, and she told me everything I had missed at school. She told me about Ms. Livi telling the class I wasn't coming back to school and how Patricia had to leave to cry in the third-floor girls' bathroom and that Dylan told her that she looked like she had little mouse eyes and that only made her cry harder. I told her I was sad that no one sang the "CHA CHA CHA!" part this year on my birthday and that I would consider letting her marry Dominic again. She told me Bubbe had knit me some socks and would I like them now? I told her she could help me feed Harvey dinner.

As Patricia and I went into the house and I began to put Harvey's food into his bowl, I tried again to get my words together. Every time I thought about it, my stomach clenched. We sat on the floor side by side and peeked in at Harvey through the cage bars. He picked up each pellet in his tiny paws and shoved them one by one into his mouth. His teeth flashed as he munched away. I stared straight ahead, trying to calm my nerves.

"Patricia, I'm sorry I got so mad at you. I know you were just trying to help, and"—I worked hard to keep my voice steady— "you really are a true friend."

Patricia ran her fingers up and down the side of the cage as she spoke.

"I wanted it to be true, too, you know, Mimi."

"I know," I said softly.

"Even if it wasn't real, putting on the show made me really happy."

"Me too."

She smiled at me then.

"And there's no way Mr. Morelli's circus could have been better than ours!"

It hurt to hear the name, but I smiled. I was pretty sure Patricia was right.

Later that night before bed, there was a slow knock at my bedroom door. I opened it to find Dominic standing there with his hands behind his back. He shifted from foot to foot, his eyes on the ground. I was surprised that he had abandoned his usual brother-at-the-door tactics in favor of a responsible Mom knock. Before my surprise had fully registered,

he pulled out a rolled-up piece of paper from behind his back and handed it to me. I unrolled it slowly. It was a large painted poster advertising a show starring "Mimi: The Most Extraordinary Mime in the World!" The title was printed in giant red block letters and in the middle of the poster was a small figure of a girl in a black and white striped T-shirt with a caramel-colored hamster sitting on her shoulder. The girl was holding colorful balloons while balancing on a tightrope. At the bottom of the poster in careful cursive was "Coming Soon." My eyes blurred with tears and I looked up at Dominic over the poster.

"Try again," he said.

EXTRA-ORDINARY	ORDINARY	EXTRAORDINARY
Dylan Weisnowski	Warm yogurt	True friends
		Original art pieces

Chapter Twenty-One

There are very many truly extraordinary things in the world. You may think otherwise, but the truth is, extraordinary things *aren't* extremely rare. They're actually everywhere! They can be hard to recognize because they can look awfully ordinary, but you should look a little closer to make sure.

I would know, too, because I invented Extraordinaryism. I'm an expert! You see, right from the moment I was born, I was extraordinary. For starters, I'm a mime. I'm not famous yet, but I will be soon. But even without fame, my life is pretty extraordinary. My family and friends always say so! And they would know a thing or two about being extraordinary, because even though I did invent Extraordinaryism, the only way I could do it was through careful observation of them.

I go to school in a brightly colored classroom that looks like a butterfly conservatory and sit next to a fluttery best friend who would crawl through vegetable gardens and sometimes even break the rules for people she loves. I have a Grandma who laughs so hard her earrings jingle and who likes to celebrate with red roses and pancake brunches. I have a mom who gives the best hugs on the whole street and loves listening to the Beach Boys in her silky work blouses. She bought me an exceptional hamster, who keeps me company and licks my tears, for my birthday, and I have a brother who is an amazing artist and amateur rocket builder who has just used his allowance to buy me a purple alarm clock. He smiles a lot more now that he has reached phase four in crossing-over.

Mostly, these people are extraordinary because they very patiently lined up outside the garage on the last evening in June before summer vacation and waited while the usher sat a series of plush guests before showing them to their seats.

I have a dad, too, and even though it's been a while since we've talked, and he wasn't in the lineup outside the garage, he is a big part of what makes me extraordinary. I guess someone can make you the extraordinary person you are but still feel extra-ordinary about themselves. At least, that's what we've decided. After all, if they can't see the extraordinary around them, how can they see it in themselves? You can't expect everyone to be an expert on Extraordinaryism. I hope we do talk again soon. Maybe then I can tell him that I wear his beret and I mime for Mom to make her laugh, just like he used to, and I can tell him about my chart, and he can see things the way I see them.

You would think with all this extraordinary around us it would be easy to feel happy all the time, but the truth is that especially without all my stories and imaginings, thinking about my dad makes me really sad. I can't help but listen harder when the phone rings, or when cars honk, and it's hard not to daydream the sad feelings away. So I'm learning to let myself feel sad. But the amazing thing is that, in letting myself feel sad, I've realized that others sometimes feel sad, too, and that makes us all feel less alone. And when I miss my dad, instead of inventing what could be, I've learned instead to remember.

"Wait! Spell it again?"

"Mimi!"

"Please, Daddy? One more time!"

"E-X-T-R-A-O-R-D-I-N-A-R-Y."

"Wow!"

"Should I keep reading?"

"Yes! But wait, will you write it down for me, too?"

Dad laughed and got up from the bed. He walked over to my desk and grabbed a purple marker.

"Here! This way you won't forget it!"

He printed it on the inside of my forearm as I giggled and squirmed.

"No! Mom says we shouldn't use markers on—"

"Almost done!" He laughed as he wrote. "I-N-A-R-Y!"

I held my arm out to examine the writing.

"You are EXTRAORDINARY." He capped the marker and smiled. "And don't you forget it!"

Most of the time, though, I try to see the extraordinary moments happening right before my eyes. Extraordinary can be found in the milk that comes out of your friend's nose when you make her laugh too hard, or in the socks Bubbe knit for you. Extraordinary is in the Christmas card your brother made you or the sound of your Grandma's snores on a rainy afternoon. It's the moment you get a neon-green cast off a newly healed arm, or a late-night cup of hot chocolate. It's the brightest blue that your tongue turns after a blue-raspberry push-up lollipop.

Sometimes, extraordinary can be easy to lose sight of. Sometimes life just goes on as usual, and maybe if you woke up on the wrong side of the bed, if it were a Monday, if someone dog-eared the pages of your favorite book, if you left one of your silkiest scarves on the subway, or if a very extraordinary thing happened to you one day in March, maybe you too would think all of these things were perfectly ordinary. Maybe you would think many of these things were even extra-ordinary. But don't be fooled. Extraordinary looks a lot like ordinary, but what makes a person extraordinary is finding the extraordinary in it.

That's the first, and only, rule of Extraordinaryism.

Curtain Call

A hush falls over the crowd as the flashlight swings around to find her. She's standing at the bottom of a skateboard ramp. She breathes in and sets her foot on the lower end of the platform.

"Ladies and gentlemen! Children of all ages! Feast your eyes upon our next act!" Her voice rings out through the garage.

"Sheeeee's fearless!"

She keeps a steady rhythm as she walks along the skateboard ramp toward the highest edge. One foot, the next. One foot, the next.

"She's nothing like you've ever seen before!"

She hears nothing but her own heartbeat. She moves slowly, arms outstretched, keeping herself balanced as she carefully steps up to the edge. She looks down at the ground to the spot where she'll land and strike her final pose. The end of her show. The moment she's worked so hard for.

"The one!"

She stops.

A memory suddenly hits her. The laughter rings in her ears, and she feels the cold portable roof, the crumpled newspaper in her hand, and the pain in her chest.

Tickticktickticktickick.

She squeezes her eyes tightly shut. She takes a deep breath. The ringing laughter fades out. The ticking timer slows. The extra-ordinary melts away. Only the extraordinary remains: a warm fuzzy ball in her hands, the swoop of the controller, a cruise boat taking flight, a brightly painted poster.

"The only!"

Standing tall, worlds above the crowd, she opens her eyes and looks around the garage at the most extraordinary of all. Grandma holds a bouquet of red roses in her lap. Mom sits in the guest of honor chair. Dominic flashes a muted smile. Patricia holds the golden hoop out in front of her, as the end-of-day June sun streams in through the open garage door. The room feels full.

A tongue-trill-drumroll splits through the air . . .

"THE EXTRAORDINARY!"

A perfect landing.

MIMI:
THE MOST EXTRAORDINARY
MIME IN THE
WORLD!

Coming Soon
directed by Patricia

Acknowledgments

I have many people to thank for their encouragement, care, and time. I am endlessly grateful to my many teachers—my elementary school teachers, English teachers, and drama teachers in particular. I will never forget your kindness and encouragement through the years. Thank you to Neil Silcox, my collaborator on *Harvey and the Extraordinary* the play, for walking alongside me through the story's beginnings. Thank you to the many who offered me their advice and guidance during this process: trusted experts Bev Cline and Derrick Chua, and astute loved ones Richard Fisher, Bailey Green, Alex Spyropoulos, Annabel Sibalis, and my partner Pete DeCourcy. I would also like to thank the many children who I've had the pleasure of working with over the years. Your imaginations inspire so much of what I create, and I credit you as my best advisers and wisest critics. Thank you to my family, friends, mentors, and kindred spirits. There are too many of you to name, and I would decorate a guest of honor chair for each and every one of you. My appreciation to Anna Bron whose illustrations brought this story to life in a way that exceeded all expectations and hopes. To the incredible team at Annick Press—all of you belong in the extraordinary column! Finally, thank you to the wonderful Claire Caldwell, who wandered into Mimi's little garage at the Toronto Fringe Festival many years ago, and without whom this book would never have happened. It has been a genuine gift.

Eliza Martin is a writer, theater artist, and arts educator.
She works with children and youth in Toronto, Ontario.
Harvey and the Extraordinary, based on her 2018 play,
is her debut novel.

Anna Bron studied traditional animation at Sheridan College.
She illustrated the award-winning picture book
Salma the Syrian Chef and has animated, designed,
and directed commercials and short films.
She lives in Vancouver, British Columbia.